W9-AGK-378

THE *HERO* OF *Ticonderoga*

DISCARDED

DISCARDED

THE HERO OF

Ticonderoga

Gail Gauthier

SCHOLASTIC INC.

New York   Toronto   London   Auckland   Sydney
Mexico City   New Delhi   Hong Kong   Buenos Aires

No part of this publication may be reproduced in whole or in part, or stored in a retrieval system, or transmitted in any form or by any means, electronic, mechanical, photocopying, recording, or otherwise, without written permission of the publisher. For information regarding permission, write to G.P. Putnam's Sons, an imprint of Penguin Putnam Books for Young Readers, a division of Penguin Putnam Inc., 345 Hudson Street, New York, NY 10014.

ISBN 0-439-49301-3

Copyright © 2001 by Gail Gauthier. All rights reserved. Published by Scholastic Inc., 557 Broadway, New York, NY 10012, by arrangement with G.P. Putnam's Sons, an imprint of Penguin Putnam Books for Young Readers, a division of Penguin Putnam Inc. SCHOLASTIC and associated logos are trademarks and/or registered trademarks of Scholastic Inc.

12 11 10 9 8 7 6 5 4   3 4 5 6 7/0

Printed in the U.S.A.   40

First Scholastic printing, December 2002

Designed by Semadar Megged
Text set in 11 pt. Berling Roman

...

For Henry Gauthier

I like oral reports that start with something lively and surprising to catch my attention. I kind of doze off through any other kind, myself. It's good to start with a quotation, too, especially if it is one of the lively and surprising kind.

> " 'Arrived at Onion River falls and passed by Ethan Allen's grave. An awful infidel, one of the wickedest men that ever walked this guilty globe. I stopped and looked at his grave with a pious horror.' The Reverend Nathan Perkins in his diary."

That was how I started my oral report on Ethan Allen, first leader of Vermont's Green Mountain Boys, winner of the battle for Fort Ticonderoga (the earliest American victory of the Revolutionary War, in case anyone cares), holder of the record for longest imprisonment of a colonial officer by the British, and local boring dead guy. I looked up at the rest of my class, whose desks were arranged in a circle around me.

They didn't look particularly lively, but they were surprised.

Other than "Thérèse LeClerc" and "April 19? 20? 18?, 1966," there was nothing else written on my paper. I wouldn't have added my name and what I thought might be the date, but I was afraid our substitute, Mr. Santangelo, would surprise me and ask to see the one paragraph I'd copied out of a library book. Since I had nothing else to read, I put my paper down on my desk, which I was very conveniently standing next to.

"Okay," I said, continuing my report. "So once Ethan knew this woman who had a toothache and needed to go to a dentist, but she was afraid of the tools he used. So Ethan said to her, 'I'll show you, madam, that losing a tooth is nothing.' He went with her to a dentist and told the guy to pull a perfectly good tooth out of his mouth. Then Ethan turned to the woman and said, 'I didn't feel a thing.' So then she let the dentist go to work on her, too.

"She was in for the shock of her life, eh?" I concluded.

I waited for the laughing to start so it wouldn't drown out the next part of my report.

I waited a little longer and looked down at Pokie's blotchy face hanging over the desk next to mine. He was to blame for my having to do the Ethan Allen report, and he knew I was mad at him. You'd think he could at least work up one of those almost laughs that end up being nothing but air coming out your nose. But, no, he just sat there looking as if he didn't quite understand what was going on.

"Once," I went on, "Ethan and one of the Green Mountain Boys (whose name I forget but it doesn't matter) were traveling along somewhere (I've forgotten where, but, again, don't worry about it). They had to spend the night out in the woods. The next morning Ethan's friend wakes up first. He looks over at Ethan and sees a rattlesnake crawling along on top of him. He wants to do something to help Ethan, but he doesn't want to scare the snake. Sure enough, it strikes Ethan. Then it strikes him again. And again and again. Finally it burps, wriggles off him, and slithers away sideways.

" 'Drunk!' the Green Mountain Boy, whoever he was, exclaims.

"That woke Ethan up. He starts to scratch at himself and says, 'Damn those mosquitoes. They're as big as horses.'

"Or cows or dogs or something. You get the point."

"Dru-u-u-nk?" Peggy Blair asked. She draws out every other word like that. It makes her sound as if she's always complaining about something. I don't know anybody who has less to complain about. "Are you saying the snake that bit Ethan Allen got drunk because Ethan Allen was drunk?"

Good ol' Peggy. She's always head of the class.

"You got the point," I told her.

"Finally," I continued, "Ethan Allen was dying. His wife called for a minister. The minister was afraid of Ethan, but he'd heard Ethan was paralyzed so he thought it was safe to speak to him.

" 'General Allen, General Allen,' he says. 'The angels are waiting for you.'

"Ethan's eyes open up and he says, 'Waiting, are they? Waiting, are they? Well, God damn 'em, let 'em wait.' "

That was my big finish, so I sat down. An oral report should have a big finish. That one did get a lot of popped eyes, a groan from Mr. Santangelo, and a suggestion that I hadn't learned the commandment about cursing in my Saturday religion classes. (That's a lie. It's most of the others I can't remember.)

"Mr. Santangelo! Mr. Santangelo!" Peggy said, her right arm waving over her head. "That wasn't an oral report. She made it all up!"

"I did not. I found every word of it in a book."

"What about beating the British at Fort Ticonderoga?" Wayne McClain asked. "That was what made him a hero."

I'd thought I had plenty of information for my report before I got to that part of the book, so I'd just stopped reading. But when Wayne asked about Fort Ti, I had this sudden feeling I might have made a mistake. I just knew that if Wayne had done the Ethan Allen report, not only would we have had to hear about Ethan beating the British, we'd also have had to listen to an account of how long it took him, the weather conditions while he was doing it, and whether he had a baked or boiled dinner when he was done.

"Everyone knows about Ticonderoga," I said, trying to sound as if I, myself, did. "I thought I would tell you some things about Ethan Allen you don't know—like how he got thrown out of town, and he got into fights with people, and . . . oh . . . here's a good story. Listen to this." I sat up straight and leaned forward a bit. "Once, while the British were holding Ethan prisoner, he had to use the outhouse. On the outhouse, there was a picture of George Washington. So—"

"When was he a prisoner?" Wayne broke in.

"And why was there a picture of George Washington on an outhouse?" Peggy asked. "They didn't have cameras back then. Where would they get a painting of George Washington? And if they had a painting—"

"You're ruining the story!" I complained. "They put a picture of George Washington on the outhouse to show they weren't afraid of him and didn't think he was much of a general. Can't you understand anything? So Ethan goes to use the outhouse, and when he comes out, he says to the British, 'Good place for that picture. Washington always did scare the crap out of you people.' "

"Give her an A!" Jack Thibodeau yelled as he began to applaud.

Mr. Santangelo lifted his head off his hands, where it had been resting since Ethan had damned the mosquitoes. "Jack, don't get started," he warned.

"Too late," Jack explained as he clapped away, the effort of bringing his great soft hands together causing him to breathe a little heavily.

I relaxed in my seat thinking I'd really saved the day with that outhouse story, toilets always being good for a laugh. Then I heard Peggy say, "See, Mr. Santangelo? It was a mistake to let Tessy do the Ethan Allen oral report. He was a hero."

"That's right," Wayne agreed. "I thought he was supposed to be like Davy Crockett or Daniel Boone. It made you feel good to think someone like that lived here once."

"Made who feel good?" I asked. "There were people who knew him who called him a heathen. He only went to church so he could fight with the minister. And . . ."

"It was the best topic and she ruined it," Peggy said. "If Mrs. Ford had been here she would never have let Tessy get up there and talk about . . . you know . . ." Peggy lowered her voice to a whisper. "C . . . r . . . a . . ."

"Abraham Lincoln told people that story about Ethan Allen and the outhouse," I objected. "If Abraham Lincoln can say . . ."

"Perhaps Thérèse did have the best topic. But that's because she is capable of being the best. All students can be the best if they're only given a chance," Mr. Santangelo explained patiently.

"Not Tessy," someone said.

"She's never been best before," Peggy reminded him.

Mr. Santangelo turned toward me. He looked a lot more tired than he had when he became our substitute teacher two weeks before. "Thérèse, your report lacked a certain narrative flow."

"A what?" half the class asked.

"It lacked order, a story line," Mr. Santangelo explained. "It was just a few stories—legends, tall tales. You hopped all over the place. First Ethan Allen was dead, then he wasn't, then he was again."

I gasped and slapped the top of my desk. "That reminds

me of something I forgot to say. Ethan's body is lost. A while after he died someone wanted to build a monument over him so they went digging to look for him, but he wasn't where they'd put him."

"This isn't helping you," Mr. Santangelo broke in.

"They think his body was stolen—maybe by medical students who wanted to use it for experiments," I finished. "It should have still been where they buried it. He drank an awful lot, and you'd think that would have preserved him for a while anyway."

"What is the point of your report?" Mr. Santangelo asked.

"What do you mean? You said I had to do it, and I did it. What do you mean, 'What is the point?' "

Mr. Santangelo took a deep breath and spoke very slowly, something he's started doing a lot lately. "Why did you choose to include those particular details in your report?"

"Because I liked them," I explained.

"I liked them, too," Jack said, with Pokie agreeing.

"It was interesting," Deborah Churchill added.

You could almost hear necks snapping as heads turned toward where Deborah was sitting quietly, running her right forefinger around the gold horse-head pin on the collar of her blouse. Deborah Churchill was interested in my oral report! The best girl in the sixth grade was interested!

"You're going to do the report again, Thérèse," Mr. Santangelo announced.

"What?" I said. Didn't he hear what Deborah had just said?

"Well, technically you're not doing it again because you didn't really do it the first time. But you're going to do an oral report on Ethan Allen. You're going to start at the beginning, and you're going to do it right. Please."

ONE

*D*eciding where things begin isn't as easy as teachers think it is. There are so many parts to any one thing, and they all have a beginning.

For instance, I could say that everything began back in second grade when I told Petie Pokornowski I'd marry him. I did it because we were the only kids in our grade to see *Invaders from Mars* on the Four O'Clock Supper Movie. He said, "Let's get married when we grow up because we like the same movies," I said, "Sure," and he spent the next four years of my life bugging me. He was always sticking his nose into my business, always hanging around, and always making trouble for me—not because he wanted to but because he's Pokie. I would never have been stuck with the Ethan Allen oral report if it hadn't been for him.

That would be a good place to begin.

Or I could say it began that year my mother had a falling out with Peggy Blair's mother when the two of them were running the 4-H Club and Mrs. Blair insisted that we all learn how to make yarn pom-poms. "For the love of God, why?" Mom had asked her right in front of all us.

It was a three-meeting ordeal that ended when Mom told Mrs. Blair that pom-poms were only good for one thing and then explained what that one thing was.

My mother and I now have nothing to do with 4-H or Mrs. Blair. There is definitely a part of this that began there.

In fourth grade Deborah Churchill moved here from New Jersey, which is another starting place. She was not a snot even though she had every right to be. She always acted as if it was an accident she got all those good grades and not as if it was because she was better than everyone else, the way some people I could mention do. Her smoky blue eyes and her dark brown hair that never fell out of its one long braid were accidents, too, as were her beautiful clothes that never got dirty or started to wear out. Deborah always acted as if being the best and most popular girl in our grade wasn't something she worked for and wanted, it was just something that happened.

From fifth grade on I kept thinking that if Peggy Blair would just go off to Catholic school the way she was always saying she was going to, I would have a chance at being friends with Deborah. With Peggy gone, it would just leave Lynn Smid and Yvette Morrissette and Tammy Boucher and every other girl in our grade and me.

Oh, yes. That was a beginning, too.

And, of course, the school year began back in September. Since that was when Mrs. Ford began to scare us with talk about how in the spring we were going to study the state of Vermont and prepare Vermont oral reports, some people might say the whole thing started then.

"Remember," Mrs. Ford would say as she handed out every worksheet, as she assigned every page of questions at the end of every unit, as she began to give us every test, "the student with the highest average in every subject gets to give the oral report on Ethan Allen, the hero of Ticonderoga."

While everyone around me scribbled like mad on their papers and wrote dozens of extra-credit book reports, I thought, I don't get it. I'm supposed to work hard so I can do some more work?

But the easiest thing to do would be to say it began on Friday, April 1, 1966, which just happened to be April Fools' Day.

On Friday, April 1, we came to school and found two of the three sections of blackboard at the front of the room had been carefully divided into squares with the word April written in cursive up above one board and May above the other. Mrs. Ford was making herself a calendar.

"Now, people," Mrs. Ford said after attendance, the Pledge of Allegiance, and the Lord's Prayer (with the Protestant "for Thine is the kingdom" part at the end, which always ticks me off because what's so hot about them that they get to have their ending on the school prayer?), "we're going to do some planning for the next month or two. What happens on Monday? Every Monday?"

No one said anything, not even the kids who always say something.

"New spelling unit, people! Where have you been all year?"

That was another question no one answered while Mrs. Ford wrote "Spelling Unit" in all the Monday squares. Then she went on to Friday and wrote "Dictation Test" on all those squares. According to Mrs. Ford's calendar, we did a new chapter of math every three weeks, a new social studies unit every two weeks, and science every Monday, Wednesday, and Thursday.

This was all news to me.

When Peggy Blair raised her hand and politely asked, "Mrs. Ford? Are you sure we do science three times a week?" Mrs. Ford turned around, pointed her chalk at Peggy, and said, "Why must you always work against me? Don't deny it! You most certainly do! Now pay attention, all of you! I'm trying to help you!"

Then she whipped around so she was facing the blackboard again and began madly writing "Unit Review," "Vermont Oral Reports," and "English Test" all over her calendars. She pounded the blackboard so hard that little bits of chalk broke off and went flying around her, sort of like the foam you sometimes see dripping off the mouth of a mad dog.

It wasn't unusual for Mrs. Ford to go on a tear, accusing this student or that student of working against her, telling us we didn't deserve her and that she didn't know why she bothered. Once, earlier in the year, she had thrown books on the floor and left the room, a really exciting event that ended badly when she came back and pretended nothing had happened. Droning on and on all morning about all the work we had to do over the next month and a half and when we were expected to do it, however, was a little odd. Except for things like the Friday dictation tests, and the Vermont stuff in the spring—which was hanging over our heads like church on Sunday—I'd always thought that we just did whatever Mrs. Ford felt like doing whenever she felt like doing it. Still, I didn't really suspect anything was up until our recess after lunch.

I had just given up trying to jump rope with a couple of fifth-grade girls who were clearly disgusted with my efforts. This left me with nothing to do and no one to do it with. Then I noticed an unusually large crowd gathered around Peggy and Deborah. Deborah was sitting on the top rail of the fence that separated the playground from the meadow next to it, watching while Peggy gabbed away to the others. So I hurried on over and stretched up over the kids at the back of the crowd to see what was going on.

"How long will she be gone?" someone was asking when I got there.

"Who? Who's going somewhere?" I asked.

"Would you please not yell all over the playground?" Peggy asked. "This is supposed to be a secret."

I looked around at the dozen or more kids listening to her. I guessed Peggy's definition of secret must be different from mine.

"Mrs. Ford is leaving for a while," Deborah explained, her voice calm and low.

"April Fool!" I shouted, thinking I was ruining a trick.

"Grow up, Tessy. This is serious," Peggy snapped. "There's something wrong with her daughter."

"What?" I asked.

"There's something wrong with her daughter," Peggy repeated as if I was some kind of idiot.

"What's . . . wrong . . . with . . . her?" I said, knowing how to talk to idiots myself.

"She's going to have a baby, and there's something wrong. Mrs. Ford is going to go stay with her so she can take care of her daughter's other children," Peggy replied. "The principal called my father last night to see if the school board would let her have time off. Mrs. Ford is very worried. We should be extra good until she leaves."

That suggestion wasn't met with much enthusiasm, but no one actually objected, either.

"But what's wrong with her daughter?" I asked once again.

"Believe me, you don't want to know," Peggy said, rolling her eyes and shaking her head.

"Yes, I do. You don't know, do you? Your father, Mr. Big Stinking Deal school board chairman, didn't tell you, did he?" I laughed.

"I know all about this sort of thing," Peggy insisted. "My mother was very sick when I was born. I almost died, you know."

It did seem as if she'd mentioned that a few hundred times.

"My mother had to stay in bed for three months before I was born," Lynn said.

"My grandmother's heart stopped when my uncle was born," one of the boys offered. "But it started again."

"*My* heart stopped when I was born," Peggy broke in.

"Doesn't that cause brain damage?" I asked.

"My older brother was born dead. He's buried in that cemetery near the grocery store. My mother has to pass it whenever she goes shopping," Yvette said. "Isn't that weird?"

We all agreed it was. Then we looked over at Peggy to see if she could top it.

She changed the subject.

"Mrs. Ford is going to be gone for weeks. I hope she decides who gets the Ethan Allen oral report before she leaves. It would be awfully hard for a substitute to decide who is the best student," she said, sounding worried.

"Why?" I asked. "Substitutes don't know how to add up grades in a grade book?"

"Maybe I'd be making jokes, too, if I knew I didn't have a chance of being chosen," Peggy said.

"What joke?" I replied as she turned her back on me. "I asked a simple question."

Peggy turned pointedly to the group of girls clustered around Deborah as if I and a couple of other kids standing near me weren't there. "Guess what? I chose the cake for my birthday party. My mother had to buy a special pan so she could make it. It's going to look exactly like one she saw in her *Good Housekeeping* magazine," she continued while the boys standing with me wandered off. "It's going to have roses made out of frosting. My mother knows how to make those."

The girl beside me left when Peggy started talking about paper cups. "They match the streamers we're going to hang in the living room.

"Tammy Boucher is the only one I invited who can't come," Peggy went on as I stood there, a little bit more to one side of her. "We're going to design the dresses we'll wear on our first dates. I've already been working on mine."

It will be a while before you get to use it . . . a long while, I thought as I noticed how really far I seemed to be from the others.

"Then we're going to make popcorn—my mother bought us Jiffy Pop—and do each other's hair."

Eavesdropping on plans for a party you're not invited to isn't all that interesting, anyway, and when Peggy got to the part about the hair I started looking around for something else to do.

Suddenly, I caught a whiff of something bad. Oh, no, I thought. Did I forget to use deodorant again? But it was just the paper mill in Ticonderoga. When the wind blows just right it brings this incredible stink from the plant in New York right across Lake Champlain. You can smell it in any number of towns in Vermont. It really gives you something to think about whenever you look at a new sheet of paper.

I looked over my shoulder at Deborah, who was still on that fence. Whenever I sat there a teacher came and told me to get off. Why? I wondered. Why was someone always looking when I was up there? Why did they always miss Deborah? Or did they? Maybe the teachers saw her up there and didn't mind. Maybe . . .

"Tessy! Tessy! Who do you think will get to do the Ethan Allen report?"

I closed my eyes and groaned. Pokie had been asking me that question every few days for the last month. Oh, how I wished someone else in our grade would talk to him.

I don't care who gets the Ethan Allen report, I almost shouted. But I stopped the words just in time because I knew Mrs. Ford had been known to shake kids who she thought were giving her lip even when she wasn't around to hear them.

"For the last time, Pokie, it doesn't matter who does the report. It's going to be just like watching reports about important people on the evening news. Are the reports any better when you watch them on Channel 3 than they are when you watch them on Channel 5?"

"I don't watch the news," Pokie said.

"Pretend you do," I continued, not letting him throw me off. "No, they are not any better. No matter who gives the report they act as if the people and things they're talking about are some really big deal when none of it matters to anybody. So somebody's going to court, somebody's passing a law, somebody's making a speech? When the next day comes nothing has changed. I still have to get up and go to school and come home and do chores. That's why I don't watch the news, either.

"And school reports on important people are even worse," I explained, "because the important people are usually *dead*, and they've been that way for a couple of hundred years, so what they did really has nothing to do with anything. So why should I care who's going to do an oral report on Ethan Allen?"

"Because all the other oral report topics are worse," Pokie replied. "You don't want to get stuck talking about dairy farmers or skiers or . . . the marble industry . . . do you?" He stopped speaking so he could shudder.

What I *wanted* to do was an oral report on how Vermonters used to freeze elderly people each fall and then thaw them out in the spring so they wouldn't die during the winter. Now, *that* would be interesting. My father had heard that people packed their parents in boxes filled with pine boughs, sealed them up, and buried them in a snowbank and left them there until there were no snowbanks. Then they woke up Granny and Granddad with a good stiff shot of one hundred proof whisky—which would wake the dead, let alone someone who was just frozen. But Mrs. Ford said she didn't care what my father had heard. So what I *planned* to do was an oral report on maple syrup. I would just cut a few pictures out of those stiff, moldy old

Vermont Life magazines stacked at the back of our classroom, glue them on a piece of cardboard, and hold it up in front of everybody. *Bada-bing, bada-bang, bada-boom*.

But poor Pokie can never do something practical like that. It's as if he looks for ways to make work for himself. He's always trying to read a book a half inch thicker than he needs to, he's always trying to do the extra-credit problems in math, he's always got his hand up even though he has to know he's going to make a fool of himself as soon as he opens his mouth.

"There's supposed to be a cave near Lake Dunmore that Ethan and his Green Mountain Boys used. I've been looking for it," Pokie said eagerly.

He would be lucky to find Lake Dunmore, forget about a cave.

"Pokie, Ethan Allen gets two sentences—two—in our social studies book. Nobody outside Vermont knows who he is. He's not worth busting a gut over."

If Pokie had an ounce of the common sense my father is so big on, he'd figure that out for himself. But Pokie doesn't seem to know what common sense is.

"I want to take pictures of the cave," he replied as if he hadn't heard a word I said. "If I don't get to do the Ethan Allen report, I'll give the pictures to Mrs. Ford. She'll love them."

I kind of doubted that.

One of the teachers started ringing the bell just then, and we all lined up to go back into the building.

"So, what was in your lunch box today, Petie Pokie?" Peggy asked while we waited to be let in. She rolled her eyes at her friends. "A great big kielbasa?"

"Kielbasa!" Jack Thibodeau repeated in this fake deep voice that he could pull out of his big chest whenever he wanted. Then he started chanting the word and doing this little dance that made his whole fat body jiggle. When he had a few of the other boys chanting with him, he stopped and gave Pokie a jab in the chest with one finger that sent Pokie stumbling against Tammy Boucher. "On Monday I expect you to share your KIELBASA with the whole class."

"I didn't have kielbasa," Pokie stammered. He had turned from his usual pale yellow color to a purple pink shade that was actually kind of scary, though no one else seemed to notice.

Jack loomed up over Pokie. "Don't lie to me, boy. I can smell KIELBASA on your breath!"

Well, I thought, there's been many a day when I'd have preferred a great big kielbasa to whatever I found waiting for me in the cafeteria. I would love to bring my lunch from home, but it's not allowed since my father thinks spending a dollar fifty a week in the school cafeteria puts us right up there with the Kennedys. Of course, if I did bring lunch, even a kielbasa, I would know not to bring it in a Bugs Bunny lunch box like Pokie does.

Here was one of those golden opportunities for me to keep my mouth shut that I always fail to take advantage of. Instead, I turned to Peggy and Jack and said, "You boobs.

He doesn't eat kielbasa on Fridays. Did you forget it's Lent? You do know what Lent is, don't you?"

Peggy is sister's pet at our Saturday morning catechism class just like she's teacher's pet at regular school. She's always afraid that if she doesn't know something, if a nun or a teacher doesn't think she, Peggy, is best, someone else will take her place. As if anyone else wants it. Lent—the weeks before Easter when Catholic kids aren't allowed to eat meat on Friday just *because*, as my mother always says—is something even Jack knows about by now. So, of course, Peggy cannot stand to have anyone think she doesn't know something like that.

And she also has a nice little fit whenever she hears the word boob.

She stood in front of everybody, huffing and puffing and sputtering while Jack looked her up and down and said he'd always wanted to see a boob. But that was all it came to. For a girl who thinks she's so smart, she isn't much of a conversationalist. Of course, sometimes you don't need to talk. Her friends all looked at me and looked at one another and nodded their heads as if they all agreed I was just the kind of person they'd expect to say boob and to say it often.

We got into our classroom, where Mrs. Ford was erasing the date from the chalkboard. She's a nice-looking person from the back, even if she is kind of old. She always wears pretty flowered dresses with matching belts. She isn't real thin, but she isn't real fat, either, and her gray permed hair looks much nicer than the gray hair of any other old person I know. From the front, though, if she took off her pointy silver-framed eyeglasses, she'd look a lot like that faded, colorless George Washington picture she keeps on the wall over her desk.

The same picture, perhaps, that the British kept on their outhouse.

"Tree-saw," was the first word out of Mrs. Ford's mouth that afternoon. And that's exactly how she always says my name. She sounds like a cartoon jackass—"Hee-haw. Tree-saw."

That morning I had been pretending to do a workbook while reading *Unexplainable Tales*, which I'd hidden under the top of my desk. *Unexplainable Tales* is full of strange but true stories, and I had been right in the middle of one about this woman sitting in a chair watching television who caught on fire for no reason (spontaneous combustion, it's called) when I'd had to stop to go to the cafeteria. So, of course, I'd gone right back to work on it after recess. Mrs. Ford was able to bray my name a couple more times while I pretended I didn't hear her so I could slip the book back into my desk.

"Tree-saw, put the date on the board for us, please."

Every morning Mrs. Ford chooses a student to put the date on the board. Then every afternoon she chooses another one to write it up there again. Kids like Peggy and Deborah are chosen in the morning. They know the date! Aren't they amazing! Kids like Pokie and Jack and me are chosen in the afternoon. We're not amazing enough to know the date at eight-thirty in the morning. For that matter, we often don't know it at twelve forty-five in the afternoon after having stared at it on the chalkboard for three and a half hours.

I went up front to take the chalk Mrs. Ford handed me. Wouldn't you know it would be one of those little, soft, grainy pieces? Then I wrote the year first, because that's the easiest. It's the same for hundreds of days, right? So I got 1966 up there with no problem. Then I wrote April. I knew it was Friday because it was Lent and not eating meat on Friday weighs heavily on my mind. That left the actual day of the month. Even if it hadn't been April Fools' Day, I couldn't miss that because Peggy was counting the days until her birthday, three weeks away.

"Mrs. Ford," Peggy called out while holding her hand up over her head. "Tessy wrote the date backward again."

Mrs. Ford sighed heavily. "Theresa, how many times do I have to tell you how we write dates? Is there something wrong with you? We write them from left to right. Do it over."

"Booby," I whispered to Peggy when I walked back to my seat.

"Mrs. Ford!" Peggy screeched, sounding really distressed. "Tessy said . . . booby!"

" 'Booby'?" Jack repeated. "What's that mean, Mrs. Ford? I don't think I know that word."

Pokie started laughing so hard he had to lie down on his desk. The boys were all looking at one another and grinning, and the girls were all red in the face with their hands clapped over their mouths so no one would know they were laughing. Still, even with all that uproar we all heard the crack as Mrs. Ford brought her ruler down on my desk.

As usual, I was too quick for her. She's never been able to hit me. Ever. Of course, she's never been able to hit anyone, though I'm a pretty big target, and Jack, being covered with all that loose flab, can't move very fast. She just makes a lot of noise as her ruler hums through the air and snaps against desks, chairs, and, sometimes, the cinderblock walls. You'd think she'd give up trying.

"How dare you people behave like this in my classroom?" Mrs. Ford demanded. "Where were you brought up that you think that is polite language—a barn?" she asked, looking at me.

She was always asking somebody that question so I knew she didn't expect me to answer her. I stared at my desk and tried to look serious.

"I hope you're ashamed of yourself," Mrs. Ford said.

We all sat silently (almost—a few people were smothering laughs at the back of the room) and waited for whatever was going to happen next.

"Well?"

I looked up at her.

"Are you ashamed of yourself?"

"Uh . . . Yes."

"I don't know why I bother with you people," Mrs. Ford

grumbled as she walked away. "I had a chance to teach in Burlington, you know. My students would have been *city* children."

We knew.

Then she turned around and snapped, "Get out a pencil and a clean sheet of paper. It's time for your dictation test."

The dictation test. That was another reason I should have remembered it was Friday. Friday is dictation day.

"I hope you all studied. Remember, the student with the highest average in every subject gets to give the oral report on Ethan Allen, the hero of Ticonderoga. You did study, didn't you, Peter?" Mrs. Ford asked, stopping to look down at Pokie. "Of course, with penmanship as bad as yours I suppose it doesn't matter. I won't be able to read your paper, anyway."

She lifted her head and smiled around the room. It was a signal that we could laugh. Smiles twitched across faces and a nervous rumble could be heard bubbling away in a few necks. Pokie sat with his pencil clutched between his teeth. I hated seeing him gnawing away on that thing like that, his eyes all pink and watery, everything about him looking little and weak.

I had to look away. I just sat at my seat, running my fingers along the smooth sides of my own pencil. It was fairly new—I didn't use it much—and the print the pencil company had stamped on the side was still fully visible.

No. 2 Ticonderoga pencil.

Ti-con-de-ro-ga. It made a great sound. Ethan Allen was just lucky he'd won a battle at such a great-sounding place, I thought as I shot a glance over at Peggy.

She was still looking very distressed over that awful word she'd had to hear. I should have been angry with her for bringing me to the attention of Mrs. Ford and her ruler. But my mother says that bad people always get punished, that sooner or later they suffer for the things they've done. I knew that in Peggy's case, Mom was right. She would get hers—for her birthday, I hoped.

TWO

We were stunned the next Monday morning when we found Mr. Santangelo in our classroom. He was not what we'd expected. He was short (which I did expect, since a lot of people have been seeming short to me lately), with lots of black curly hair, dark-framed glasses, and a brown checked jacket that he wore every day over one of a number of long-sleeved sweaters. Whenever he took the jacket off, without fail, one of his elbows was coming through a sweater sleeve—sometimes both of them. The knot of his tie just poked out over the top of those ratty sweaters, and the socks we glimpsed between his corduroys and his shoes rarely matched.

All of which was really small potatoes compared with the fact that Mr. Santangelo was . . . A MAN! There had never been one in our school who wasn't there to fix something. Well, maybe one of the bus drivers might have come in once or twice for some reason. But if he did, he didn't stay long. My older brother had had some men teachers at the high school, but it was for shop and math, for crying out loud. Man stuff. They didn't teach things like the major crops in Nebraska or how to tell the difference between an adverb and an adjective.

But Mr. Santangelo didn't seem at all worried about being able to manage the job. He sat down on the corner of Mrs. Ford's desk, crossed his legs, and started right in telling us the story of his life.

We sat there gawking while he told us about going to a bunch of different schools, hitchhiking in Alaska, tutoring poor children in Philadelphia, and writing a play that had two performances in a church somewhere in New York. When he got started on describing the papers he'd written in college, I pulled *Unexplainable Tales* out of my desk and read two whole chapters.

"Tessy," Yvette Morrissette hissed and gave me a poke in the shoulder that may have been meant to be friendly, but I don't think so. "It's your turn."

My turn for what?

"We're all getting to know one another," Mr. Santangelo said. "Would you like to stand up and tell us a little bit about yourself?"

What I would like to have done was keep reading my book while they went on without me. But instead I stood up and said, "I'm Tessy LeClerc. Uh . . ."

"Tessy . . . is that short for Theresa?" Mr. Santangelo asked.

"Thérèse."

"Oh! How beautiful! Do you guys know how lucky you are to have a French culture all around you? Why, one summer . . ."

I had never noticed anyone acting as if they felt particularly lucky to have my family around them. Or the Morrissettes, Bouchers, LaFontaines, or any of the other French families who had moved down here when my grandparents came from eastern Ontario after World War I. And as for Jack's family, the Thibodeaus? A lot of people just plain don't like them.

But even if Mr. Santangelo had known any of that, it probably wouldn't have stopped him from going off on a story about picking grapes in the south of France, leaving me free to read half an unexplainable tale about someone who answered the telephone one day and ended up having a conversation with her dead grandfather.

When we came in from the morning recess, Mr. Santangelo had moved our desks from the straight lines Mrs. Ford and every other teacher in our school liked so much into a big circle. This was terrific because you didn't have to turn around to talk to people. And, we found out later, you could throw things and hit anyone in the room with hardly any effort at all. Mr. Santangelo smiled and watched us all hunting for our desks while he sat on top of Mrs. Ford's.

Then he said, "I want to make one thing very, very clear. . . ."

Oops, I thought. Here comes trouble.

"This is not my classroom. It is ours."

We just sat there looking at him. Mrs. Ford had always made very, very clear that the classroom was hers, and as far as I was concerned, she could have it.

"Does anyone know what I mean by that?" Mr. Santangelo asked.

Deborah slowly raised her hand. "In the school I went to in New Jersey it meant we got to sit wherever we wanted to."

"Yes!" roared Jack. "Yes! Yes!"

And he shoved his desk halfway across the room and started pulling himself along in his chair to reach it.

"No! No!" Mr. Santangelo said as Wayne McClain made a space for Jack, and Peggy, Lynn, and Yvette started pulling their desks over toward Deborah. Pokie gave me a big grin and started heading my way.

"Okay, then," Mr. Santangelo agreed as desks and chairs shot back and forth across the room.

When we were done, Peggy reminded Mr. Santangelo that it was time for someone to rewrite the date on the chalkboard.

"Let's write a line of poetry up there instead," he suggested. "I thought we'd have a poetry discussion every afternoon after lunch."

"Every afternoon?" Pokie asked.

"Sure. Who has a line they'd like to share?"

"We usually do spelling on Monday afternoons," one of the girls said.

Not that Monday afternoon.

We didn't have current events the next afternoon, either. First we had our poetry discussion, the only part of which I remember is Mr. Santangelo asking, "What do you suppose Langston Hughes meant when he said '. . . fester like a sore—and then run?' in 'Dream Deferred'?"

"Fester?" Jack repeated. "That's the uncle in *The Addams Family*!"

The discussion ended soon after that, and we had to write essays on what was important to us.

"What do you mean by important?" Peggy asked after we were given the assignment. "How important? Very important or just something we like?"

"Well . . ." Mr. Santangelo said uncertainly.

"She means should this be about something we're *supposed* to think is important, like an end to the war in Vietnam, or should it be about something we *really* think is important, like being allowed to stay up later on school nights," Deborah explained.

"Ah. I think you should decide that."

My essay was about how I thought it was important that I not write an essay about something important. Even though I threw in an extra paragraph about how the classroom was "ours" and I didn't remember anyone asking me if I wanted to write this essay in "our" classroom, the whole thing came to only half a page.

"My father says Mr. Santangelo's married," Peggy said to Deborah and Lynn at lunch on Friday. "His wife is still in college."

I was sitting at the next table playing with my shepherd's pie because I certainly wasn't going to eat it. I could hear the girls discussing how long Mr. Santangelo might have been married, where he could have met his wife, what she might look like, and where they could possibly live. I set to work squashing my foam cake—if it was cake—into my shepherd's pie and casually draping my paper napkin over the whole mess. By the time I was finished, the boys at the other end of my own table were deep into a serious talk about Mr. Santangelo's bicycle, how tall it was, how much it weighed, and whether it was made in Italy or France.

Speak of the devil, as they say, and he appears. It was Mr. Santangelo, himself, who came through the cafeteria ringing the bell announcing the end of lunch period. I leaped to my feet. That was a little trick I had learned. If I rushed to clean my tray into the big trash cans before a teacher could catch sight of it, she couldn't force me to stay in from recess to eat the nourishing food my parents had paid good money for. Another good trick was to keep my head down so I wouldn't notice someone catching sight of me. That's what I was doing when I ran into Mr. Santangelo.

"What's the hurry?" he asked as he grabbed my tray to keep it from spilling all over him. "The garbage cans aren't going anywhere."

"True," I said as I watched him suddenly turn and rush off to break up a fight between Jack and three fourth graders who, Jack said, had called him fat.

"When do we find out about the Ethan Allen reports?" Wayne asked Mr. Santangelo right after lunch.

"Ethan who?" Mr. Santangelo replied.

"I told you no one had heard of him outside Vermont," I whispered to Pokie. We were well aware that Mr. Santangelo had lived in many fascinating places, but he'd only been in Vermont since Christmas.

"My mother took me to the library last night," Peggy announced eagerly.

"What do you want . . . a medal?" Jack snorted.

Peggy held up a book with heavy green front and back covers that together were nearly as thick as the pages they held between them. "I wanted a book on Ethan Allen, and the librarian says this is the best one."

"They have more than one?" I asked.

"Oh, sure," Peggy said in one of those "How could you even ask?" tones. "But *Ethan Allen: Our Hero* is the most appropriate one for people our age."

"What are you doing with it?" Pokie wanted to know.

"I don't want to wait until the last minute to get started on the report," Peggy explained. "And I don't want to have to do it on the weekend of my birthday party."

"Why do you think you're going to get to do your report on Ethan Allen?" Jack demanded.

"Well, come on . . . it's either going to be Wayne, Deborah, or me."

"Have you been keeping track of everybody's averages?" Jack argued.

She didn't have to. I hadn't been keeping track, and I knew it was going to be Peggy, Deborah, or Wayne.

"Wait just a minute," Mr. Santangelo broke in. "I was

told I'd be getting a letter from Mrs. Ford about oral reports in a couple of days, so I'm not clear on what's going on here. Are you saying this assignment is given to the winner of a competition? You guys have been competing against one another?"

Mr. Santangelo groaned and shook his head. "No wonder our schools are in such a sad state of affairs," he said, sounding a whole lot like he was announcing that someone had been shot.

"It's okay, Mr. SanTan," Jack said, gently waving his hands up and down in front of himself in a calming gesture. "It's just a talk that most of us are going to get Cs and Ds on. It's nothing to get upset about."

The idea of Jack being nice and thoughtful to anyone is just really, really funny, so, of course, some of us started to laugh. Jack gave us a big grin, and then said, "You need to take a load off, Mr. Santangelo. Why don't you just sit down in your chair . . ."

"It's Mrs. Ford's chair," Peggy pointed out, which is something she's always doing—correcting people when they've said something wrong. Only just then it was kind of funny, so some more people started laughing. Then, of course, Pokie had to start laughing really hard and something came up out of his nose, which was hysterical. And the whole thing ended with Mr. Santangelo erasing Mrs. Ford's calendars from the chalkboard because he said they tied him down too much and kept us from being creative, which was probably true since we didn't know what he was talking about.

"I got a letter from Mrs. Ford on Friday afternoon," Mr. Santangelo announced first thing on the Monday morning of his second week with us. "And there was another one waiting for me this morning." He didn't sound very happy about it.

"Burn them!" Jack shouted.

"Jack," Mr. Santangelo said in a low, kind tone. "You probably don't realize it, but your voice is very loud. You need to work on being quieter. Would you do that? Would you?"

"Sure!" Jack bellowed.

"Good." Mr. Santangelo looked down at a paper in his hand. "Now this whole business about studying the state of Vermont sounds very interesting. I thought maybe we could try to arrange for a field trip while we're working on it. What's the general feeling about that?"

The general feeling wasn't good.

"Are you going to make us go to the cemetery again?" Pokie asked.

"What do you mean again? You went on a field trip to a cemetery?"

"Several times," I told him.

"Every spring each grade brings flowers and flags to a different cemetery so we can decorate the graves of dead soldiers," Peggy explained.

"Of course we decorate the graves of *dead* soldiers," Jack sneered. "Who's ever heard of a *live* soldier having a grave?"

"I can't believe this," Mr. Santangelo said, holding one hand to his forehead.

"It's not a bad field trip," Peggy said, trying to sound enthusiastic, because, as we all knew, her mother was the main reason we had to make the cemetery circuit every year.

"Yes, it is," Jack insisted.

"When I lived in New Jersey, we went on field trips to museums and farms and to see plays. Couldn't we do something like that?" Deborah asked.

"I don't want to go to a farm!" Yvette wailed. "I live on a farm!"

"I'll think of something," Mr. Santangelo promised. "Now, Mrs. Ford says you're supposed to make Vermont notebooks, and that you know what you're supposed to put in them."

"No, we don't!" I exclaimed.

"Mrs. Ford's been talking about it all year," Peggy objected, rolling her eyes at me. "Of course we know what we're supposed to do."

"I don't," I insisted.

Mr. Santangelo picked up Mrs. Ford's plan book and stood in front of his desk holding it in one hand and her letter in the other. "This could be good," he said, sounding doubtful. "Everyone works independently so no two notebooks will be the same. . . ."

"Can Jimmy and I work together?" Jack shouted.

"Oh, that's a good idea," Lynn agreed. "Can Yvette and I work together, too?"

"No, no," Mr. Santangelo said. "I want everyone to have an opportunity to express themselves. I want to learn about you as individuals. I want . . ."

"*I* want to work with you," Tammy complained to Lynn.

"But I've already said I'd work with Yvette. Sorry. Maybe you can work with Peggy," Lynn suggested.

"I'm working by myself," Peggy said quickly.

"I'm not working with anybody," I called over to them, a big smile on my face, a hint in my voice.

Lynn leaned over to Tammy. "Yvette and I will let you work with us," she whispered.

"Oh, okay, then," Mr. Santangelo agreed as kids ran around the circle, desperately trying to attach themselves to someone.

I saw Deborah looking at me, smiling. She was by herself, no partner. And she was smiling at me. I nodded my head encouragingly at her, meaning, "Sure, I'll be your partner." We'd do a notebook together, we'd be friends, I'd get to hang around at recess with the neatest girl in our grade.

Suddenly I was looking down at Pokie, who, for some reason known only to himself, was lying across my desk.

"We'll work together, huh?" he was saying, his little pasty face turned up toward mine. It was a question, but it wasn't really a question. You could tell he was expecting only one answer.

When I looked back toward Deborah, Wayne McClain was standing next to her desk and the two of them were looking at a piece of paper together—lists of what each of them was going to do on their Vermont notebook, as it turned out.

It all happened so fast, it just took my breath away.

"When do we find out about our oral report topics?" Peggy asked.

"Yeah! The oral reports!" a half dozen voices repeated.

Mr. Santangelo looked down at the plan book, a frown on his face. "Oral reports are good. They build confidence and speaking skills."

"Who cares?" Jack called out. "What about Ethan Allen?"

"The smartest kid in the class gets to do the Ethan Allen oral report," Peggy explained. "That's what Mrs. Ford said. It's a reward for being smart."

"That's not you, then," Jack snapped at her.

"I get the best grades."

Pokie pointed at Wayne. "Wayne gets the best grades! Wayne should get to do the report."

Mr. Santangelo closed his eyes and dropped the plan book on the desk. Actually, it was a little more than a drop, but not quite a throw. Maybe Jack was right and Mr. Santangelo should have burned Mrs. Ford's letters. It looked as if he might be catching something from her.

"How many times do I have to tell you guys! Grades have nothing to do with learning! Doing whatever you have to do to get a grade isn't learning anything!"

Grades were one of Mr. Santangelo's favorite things to talk about after poetry and the hundreds of cool things he'd done. He often accused us of just repeating what we'd been told, refusing to think for ourselves, and trying to guess what he wanted us to say in order to get an A or a B. All of which seemed like a lot of effort to me.

"I *will not* reward anyone for getting good grades," he continued. "Good work, yes. But not good grades."

"I do good work," a half dozen people called out.

"So do I."

"Me, too."

"I know I do good work because I get good grades," Peggy insisted, sounding close to tears.

Mr. Santangelo waved his hands and shouted, "Listen, everybody" two or three times until the teacher next door finally came in and our class quieted down.

"This is what I'm going to do." He dumped the contents of Mrs. Ford's pencil holder onto the desk. "If you want to do the oral report on this Ethan Allen person, write your name on a little piece of paper and put it in here. You better make it really little. Then I'll pull a name out, and that person gets to do the report."

"Well, that's not fair!" Peggy howled.

"And just giving you the report is?" Jack said.

"It would be fairer."

"We're doing it this way so everyone gets a chance— the same chance. Everyone is going into this equal. If you want to be considered, get your paper in fast. I'm going to pull out a name in just a few minutes and then this whole discussion will be over," Mr. Santangelo announced.

I sat back and watched as everyone around me madly

tore up papers, scribbled on them, crumpled them, and started again. I knew Jack put his name in twice, but I didn't say anything because it would be fun to see Jack, who stayed back one year and should have stayed back another, win something away from Peggy and Wayne.

"Is everyone ready?" Mr. Santangelo asked.

"No! No!"

"Wait!"

Mr. Santangelo sighed and held the pencil holder out in front of him so two more people could jam their papers in.

"Ready? Okay. I am going to draw out a name. I'm going to read it. Then we will go on to other things."

Mr. Santangelo paused and grinned. "I think it's really marvelous that you people are so enthusiastic about this oral report. Your interest in learning is very inspiring."

"The losers are going to have to do talks on different types of sap buckets," Wayne explained glumly.

"Perhaps someone could write a poem about sap buckets," Mr. Santangelo said as he pulled out a little piece of paper. He slowly put the pencil holder down and held the paper up to his face.

"This is very good," he said, nodding. "I'm very happy that this person won."

A hopeful smile twitched at the corners of Peggy's mouth.

"The Ethan Allen oral report goes to . . . Thérèse LeClerc," Mr. Santangelo announced.

He was smiling at me as Peggy and I shouted, "No!"

"I don't want it!" I said.

"Then why did you put your name in?" Mr. Santangelo asked impatiently.

"I didn't. I want to talk about sap buckets."

"I put her name in," Pokie explained. "We're partners on the Vermont notebook. I figured she wanted her name in."

"I want it!"

"Give it to me!"

"Tessy, give it to me!"

The teacher from the next classroom opened our door and stuck her head in again.

"Tessy isn't giving anything to anybody. We could go on arguing about this for the rest of the year. But we're not going to. The report is hers. Besides, I think it will be a good experience for you," Mr. Santangelo assured me.

I didn't see how.

THREE

"*R*un, Tessy, run!" my brother, Marcel, yelled as soon as the school bus pulled away from the two of us the next afternoon. "The LaFontaines' dog is loose again."

The road and yard in front of our house are incredibly flat, and I couldn't see a sign of so much as a squirrel, let alone our neighbor's man-eating cur. But I didn't spend too much time looking. If you could actually see ol' Brownie, it was probably too late to do more than say your prayers.

I slipped and slid across the slick layer of hardened snow that covered the lawn under our row of leafless maple trees but made better time as I ran around the house. I was gasping as I stumbled up the steps to the screened-in back porch. Marcel stood on the other side of the door, holding it shut.

"Let me in! Let me in!" I screamed.

"He's going to get you! Brownie's going to get you!" Marcel shouted, a little too gleefully it seemed to me.

My mind was already beginning to work out what was

going on but not in time to keep my hand from pounding on the wooden frame of the door.

"The chickens are all inside in this weather, and he's already killed every rabbit for miles around. He's desperate, Tess. He's got to try to bring down bigger game."

"Very funny, Marcel."

"Can you feel his breath on the back of your legs? Is he getting dog slobber on you?"

"It must have taken you days to plan this. Did you get help?" I asked calmly.

"You should have seen yourself." Marcel laughed. "You've never run that fast in your whole life, have you?"

"Ah, I wasn't even trying."

Suddenly, Marcel's eyes grew large as if he could see something behind my shoulder.

"Give up and let me in, Marcel. I'm not going to fall for it again. I'm not you, you know."

Marcel threw himself at the screen door, shoving it open against me and knocking me off the step. He didn't let it close. Instead, he stepped out, grabbed my coat, and pulled me onto the porch. I was on the floor when he pulled the door shut just in time for a giant brown creature to throw itself against it. By the time it started to growl, its open mouth desperately trying to get hold of the screening, we were both in the kitchen with a more solid door slammed shut behind us.

Deborah Churchill's family dog was an Irish setter, and Peggy Blair's was supposed to be a collie, though it was a little on the fat and short side for a collie if you ask me. The LaFontaines' dog, Brownie, wasn't anything but mean. If Brownie was on his chain, he would jerk himself off his feet lunging at anyone who came into his yard. If he was locked in a shed, you could hear him in there frantically banging against the door. Once Mr. LaFontaine tied him to an old Flexible Flyer sled he'd found at the dump, trying to keep him nearby while giving him some air. Brownie was seen dragging it down the road on his way to make trouble for one of the neighbors. Dogs are supposed to go bad once they've had the taste of blood. Brownie tasted plenty and somewhere along the line he sampled man and decided he liked it. He was always looking for more. Brownie was the reason we never begged our parents for a dog. After being chased by him once or twice, we were happy to settle for Gimpy, our old three-legged barn cat.

"Where's Dad?" Marcel asked, looking out the back window toward the barn.

Someone had brought the mail in and dropped it on the kitchen table. I held up a note that had been written on the back of an envelope from the Ethan Allen Insurance Company.

" 'Taking Aunt Joséphine to doctor. Dad gone to buy hay. Back soon. Mom,' " I read aloud.

"Damn. He said he'd kill that dog the next time it came in our yard. It'll probably be gone by the time he gets back," Marcel said as he took the envelope away from me.

"Mr. LaFontaine said he'd call the police if Dad killed Brownie," I reminded him.

"Yeah," Marcel said with a smile.

Then he waved the envelope in front of me. "Don't you love the way Mom always puts her name at the end of these little messages she leaves for us? She must be afraid that if she doesn't sign them you'll go nuts trying to guess who wrote it."

"*You* might go nuts trying to figure that out. *I* can recognize my own parents' handwriting when I see it," I told him.

"When have you ever seen Dad's handwriting?" Marcel sneered as he took advantage of Mom's not being home to cut himself a quarter of a leftover cake. "When has he ever written a note—or anything else—to anyone? If there's any writing done here, Mom always does it."

He looked up at me. "You know, the old man didn't go to high school. I bet he doesn't know how to write."

"Of course he knows how to write. I'm not stupid."

"I'm not saying *you're* stupid. I'm saying *Dad* is. Admit it . . . you've never even seen him hold a pencil, have you?"

"If Dad ever hears you saying he's stupid, you know what he'll do to you, don't you?" I reminded him. I picked up the new *Vermont Catholic Tribune* off the kitchen table and started turning the pages.

Marcel made a halfhearted attempt to hide the knife he used to cut the cake as well as some crumbs and icing. "This really ticks me off. He's making me finish high school, and he can't even write us a note telling us he went to buy hay."

"Why don't you ask him if he can write?"

"Because I want to live long enough to finish high school," Marcel said as he left the kitchen.

"Which ought to take you another five or six years," I muttered as I studied the movie section of the church paper. I love the list of films under the heading "Morally Objectionable for All." The titles don't tell me very much, but I never give up hoping.

The string beans my mother had canned in August looked a whole lot less like food and a whole lot more like some mad scientist's jarred specimens after sitting in our cellar for the past eight months. But we had to eat them anyway, so I was heating up beans on the stove late that afternoon when Mom and I suddenly heard my father call to us, "Listen, you!" He was standing in the doorway to the porch, pointing toward the pink clock radio covered with bits of dried cake and pancake batter on the shelf over the sink.

" '. . . WIPS, Ticonderoga, New York,' " a chipper group of people finished singing. And then a sober voice announced, " 'In the shadow of the great stone fortress.' "

"I love the way that sounds, me." Dad sighed as Marcel pushed his way past him and hurried over to wash his dirty hands all over the clean dishes our mother had left in the sink.

We knew Dad loved the Ticonderoga radio station's slogan about the old fort, just like we know he loves it when Walter Cronkite says, "And that's the way it is . . .," at the end of the *Evening News;* when Scarlett O'Hara says, "Tomorrow is another day," at the end of *Gone with the Wind;* when Elvis Presley sings, "Some things were meant to be" anywhere in "Can't Help Falling in Love." How could we not know? When he first hears something he might like, he repeats it, as if he's tasting the words. Once he's decided he likes what he's said, he repeats it a few times—sings it if it's a song—until he has it memorized.

"Why don't you just write it down?" I asked him once.

"What good would that do?" he replied. "I don't like the way it looks, I like the way it sounds."

Dad ran his hand—neither of which he'd washed yet after doing who knows what in the barn for the last couple of hours—through the short hair at the back of my neck and said, "Ça va, Bébé Thérèse?" He rolled the *r* in "Tairace" so hard I could imagine his tongue vibrating in his mouth, and he ended the word with a soft hiss. Those *r*s— and the words repeated for emphasis and the way he turns sentences into questions sometimes—are a sure sign he spoke only French until he started grade school. My uncles, Jack Thibodeau's father—they all talk like that.

"Okay," I replied.

"It's only okay for you today, eh? What's the matter?"

"Well," I admitted, "Peggy Blair is having a party next week, and she didn't invite me."

"I hate to imagine what a party at the Blairs' house must be like," Mom sneered.

Dad was more sympathetic. "What do you want to go to the Blairs' ritzie-poopie party for? You can't have any fun there," he said as he cleaned and dried his hands. "You know what you should do, you? Have a party and don't invite the Blair girl. She'd be the sorry one then."

The only way Peggy and her crowd would be sorry

about any party of mine would be if they came, I thought as I plopped the pan of pulpy old beans onto the table. We couldn't even scrape together enough matching plates and cups for our family to eat off of, forget about trying to co-ordinate anything with streamers. And as far as cakes from *Good Housekeeping* were concerned . . . well, let's just say we don't get that magazine here. Nope, we are not *Good Housekeeping* types.

Marcel watched Mom pull a big bowl out of the oven. "Macaroni and cheese again?" he complained.

"It's Friday," Mom reminded him.

"God doesn't mean a man to go without meat," Dad grumbled as he spooned a great wad of paste out of the bowl and onto his plate. Dad always thinks he has a better idea of what God means a man to do than, say, the priest who runs our church. "Ah, but He watched out for me today, Him, when I tipped my truck over."

"Roland!" Mom gasped. "Why didn't you say something?"

"I *am* saying something. I tipped it over in front of Paul Thibodeau's place. A cat ran out in the road. I'm turning the wheel, me, so I don't hit it, and the next thing I know, I'm sitting like this. . . ."

He paused so he could tip the top part of his body sideways while clutching an imaginary steering wheel with both hands.

"The truck landed on the passenger side, so I'm in the air holding on to the steering wheel for dear life so I don't drop."

"What did you do?" I asked.

"I dropped," Dad explained, extending his arms like a ballerina's, "like a snowflake . . . so I don't break nothing. The window, I mean."

Marcel laughed. "How did you get out?"

"Paul, him and Junior climbed up on the driver's side of the cab and got the door open so I can climb out. Then the three of us, we tipped the truck back up on its wheels. I got back in the truck and drove away."

Dad grinned. "Ol' Paul, he looks at me and says, 'Next time—hit the cat!'"

My father's life seems to be full of little stories like that, complete with punch lines. Marcel and I laughed, and my mother said that God watched out for those who didn't watch out for themselves. "It could have been worse," she added.

"Oh, yeah," Dad said. He winked at me. "It could have happened *after* I loaded the truck with hay. I wouldn't have wanted to lift those bales twice, eh? Makes a man think."

Dad's truck has a big bed in back with side racks that go up to my shoulders because he carries other farmers' milk cans into the processing plant every morning after he finishes his own chores. I wouldn't want to have to put anything in the back of that truck even once.

Mom smiled and got up to pour coffee for Dad and herself. "I think I would have preferred loading a truck with hay twice to sitting in a doctor's waiting room with Aunt Joséphine."

"Tante Joséphine is a wonderful woman," Dad said as

he dived into the sugar bowl with his spoon. "How's she doing?"

"She has gas," Mom said just before she popped a fork full of macaroni into her mouth.

Marcel hooted and hollered, and Dad paused in the middle of stirring his coffee. "And how do you know that, you?" he asked.

"Because she told me. And she told the doctor's receptionist. And she told the man sitting next to her. And she told two women sitting on the other side of the room. I tried to change the subject. I asked her if she was planning to have a garden this year. 'Oh, non, non,' she said. 'Ever'ting I eat, it give me gas. Why boter?' So I asked her if she's going to Michel's wedding. 'Oh, if I can do somet'ing about dis gas, mebbe.' "

Only one of my mother's parents speaks French, so she never learned to speak it herself. But she can do a very good imitation of her father's sisters, right down to the way their voices keep rising and falling in a sort of rhythm, making everything they say sound like singing.

"Three times I heard the story about how when she was at Fanny Allen Hospital last year there was a nurse who knew what to do for her, who knew how to get rid of gas. 'If I could jus' fin' dat woman, me.' It was unbelievable," Mom concluded. "Just unbelievable."

Unbelievable, Mom? I thought. Unbelievable? What's unbelievable is that you're talking about this at the kitchen table while I'm trying to eat my supper. No wonder I can't get an invitation to a decent birthday party.

I poured ketchup on my macaroni and cheese and went over once again the evidence I had to support my hope that I was adopted. It was the only way I could think of that would explain how I ended up with these people.

No one would guess that I was related to Dad and Marcel. That's a comfort. They are both short and scrawny, with no guts and no backsides. They have square chins and broad foreheads, Marcel's topped with a dark brown crew-cut and Dad's with long brown hair slicked back when it isn't all messed up from wearing a Blue Seal Feed cap. Everyone says I look like my mother, but everyone is wrong, wrong, WRONG! I'm already as tall as she is, and she's only as tall as my father. I'm going to tower over both of them. I don't have her big Bambi eyes or her little pointed chin. And I'm not as fat as she is. Not that Mom's really fat, just fat the way everybody's mother is fat. So I absolutely do *not* look like her.

I am nothing like them. My face . . . well, my face doesn't actually have a real shape. And I have trouble deciding what color my hair is. My body is very unusual because absolutely nothing looks good on it, which makes me feel a lot better about the fact that all my clothes are hideous. It would be a shame to waste nice things. As for—

"What did you think when that dog actually showed up?" Marcel was suddenly asking me, his face all crinkled up with laughter.

I had missed his story of Brownie's sudden appearance in our yard.

"I'm going to kill that dog, me, I'm going to kill it," Dad growled from between his clenched jaws as he slapped the table.

I hear this a couple of times a week, which is either boring or upsetting depending on how he says it and what mood I'm in. I would love to hear that ol' Brownie had gone on to doggie heaven. I wouldn't miss him a bit. I'm just not crazy about the idea of my father being the one to send him there. Sure, Dad kills chickens and the occasional pig or cow, but we eat those. But killing a dog? It's a little too close to being a murderer, if you ask me.

"How's the new teacher?" Mom asked me. Her voice was friendly, but she had a warning look on her face.

I took the hint and said, "Great!"

"No, no, no. You two are always doing this to me. You think I'm going to forget that dog is crazy mad because you're talking about something else? No! I am going to k—"

"I'm doing the Ethan Allen oral report," I said suddenly. "I got picked yesterday. The new teacher picked me."

That did the trick. Everyone was silent and looking at me.

"But you said that report would go to . . ." Mom stopped awkwardly.

". . . the smartest kid in the class," Marcel finished. "Mrs. Ford always gives it to the kid with the best grades. Then the slow kids have to do reports on things like town meetings or why maple leaves turn red in the fall."

I smiled and shrugged.

"What happened?" Marcel asked suspiciously. "Did this new teacher draw names out of a hat or something?"

I didn't have to answer that because Dad had jumped up and was planting a big smooch on the side of my head.

"Your sister is a smart girl," he told Marcel. "You saw all the Cs on her last report card, eh?"

Marcel and I looked at each other and then quickly looked away. He didn't dare make a crack about my Cs. He wished he had a report card that good.

"So when do you give this report?" Mom asked.

"Monday."

Dad had finished eating and was lighting up a cigarette. "What are you going to say?" he asked as he blew out a long stream of smoke.

"Uh . . . I don't know."

"What did your teacher tell you to do?" Mom asked.

"He said we should all do whatever we wanted to. He said that was when the best kinds of learning take place."

"I wish I had a teacher like that," Marcel said while Mom and Dad looked suspicious.

"He doesn't believe in bad grades," I explained, in part to really rub it in to Marcel and in part to make my parents forget about my report, which they would never have known about if I hadn't been trying to make my father forget about killing the neighbor's dog. "He gave me a B on the first essay he assigned us."

"A B!" they all repeated.

"He wrote, 'I admire the way you get right to the point,' in red across the bottom of the paper."

There were some more exclamations from my family.

"He told Pokie he was very imaginative, and he told Peggy he admired the strength of her feelings. It's all she can talk about now—how strong her feelings are."

"She must have some strong feelings about not getting to do this report," Mom said. "She always gets the best of everything from the teachers."

"She had her mother call Mr. Santangelo last night," I told her.

"What did Brenda tell him?" Mom asked. "That her husband is the school board chairman and a *licensed* plumber so her daughter should get the Ethan Allen report?"

"Whatever it was, it didn't work. Peggy's doing her oral report on the University of Vermont."

"I like this Mr. Santangelo. He sounds like a man with common sense. You think so, too?" Dad asked.

Actually, I didn't, since I understood common sense to mean a person who was wise and practical and I didn't think a wise, practical person would let me within shouting distance of the Ethan Allen report. On the other hand, it was nice to think that a wise, practical person wouldn't let Peggy do it, either.

"I guess," I said, answering Dad without having to give an opinion one way or the other. "Except, I really don't want to do this report. I can't find any pictures of Ethan. I know they didn't have cameras back then, but you'd think that if he was all that famous somebody would have painted him. A good oral report should be mostly pictures, you know."

Dad seemed to understand, but Mom wasn't convinced.

"Then you'll have to read a book, Tessy," she said.

"About Ethan Allen?"

"That's what the report is about, isn't it?"

"Maybe you should call Mr. Santangelo and complain about the oral report assignments, too. Maybe if both you and Mrs. Blair complain, he'll give the Ethan Allen report to Peggy and I can do something that I can find pictures for," I suggested.

"Just a minute," Dad said as he waved his cigarette at me. "The Blairs, they all think they fart between their shoulder blades, them, because they're too good to do it the way everybody else does, right?"

"Right!" Mom said quickly. Was she ever going to get over the pom-pom thing at 4-H?

"And their girl . . . she thinks she should do this report because she's better than our Thérèse, right?"

"I don't mind," I said, sounding pretty weak.

Dad's cigarette nodded at me. "You're doing that report, you."

And so I did.

• • •

That is how I ended up giving the Ethan Allen oral report. The whole thing would have been over in just a few minutes, and I would have sat down with at least a C, and maybe better since Mr. Santangelo is opposed to bad grades, if it hadn't been for Peggy. It was all her fault.

Actually, it was doubly her fault because, first, she took the only "appropriate" Ethan Allen book for people our age out of the town library, and, second, she didn't return it.

That, of course, just left "inappropriate" books for me to use for my report. Look up "inappropriate" in a dictionary. It *should* tell you that the word means stories about drinking stonewalls (rum diluted with hard cider—evidently a real taste treat in days of old) and taking the name of the Lord in vain whenever you get a chance and lifting bags of salt with your teeth and throwing them over your head. That last part is another thing Ethan Allen is supposed to have done. I left it out of my oral report because I liked the dentist story better, and I thought one tooth tale was enough.

I don't like to repeat myself.

And that was just the stuff I found while I was skipping around in one of the three "inappropriate" books the library had. I could have come up with a lot more if I'd had the guts to actually sit down and read something like, say, *The Narrative of Colonel Ethan Allen's Captivity* by the old boy himself.

"There was none of that kind of thing in the book on Ethan Allen that *I* read," Peggy said after Mr. Santangelo announced I'd have to do my report again.

"Then you read the wrong book," Jack told her.

"I don't think so," she objected as she took *Ethan Allen: Our Hero* out of her desk where it had evidently been safely stored all the time I'd been doing my research. She smiled an evil little smile, and I repeated over and over to myself, bad people get punished, bad people get punished.

FOUR

"What do you mean . . . I should be grateful?" I yelled at Peggy during recess that same day. "I didn't ask to do my oral report on Ethan Allen!"

"It doesn't matter whether or not you asked for it! You got it!" Peggy yelled back. "And look what you did with it!"

"Some people liked what I did with it," I pointed out.

"Jack?"

"Deborah, too," I reminded her.

"She just said that so she'd sound nice."

You could tell Peggy thought she'd come up with a huge insult with that one, but it backfired big time. Ha! I wanted Deborah to sound nice when she was talking about me.

"You didn't even mention that Ethan's brother, Ira, gave land for the University of Vermont to be built on," Peggy complained.

"Even if I wanted to put something boring like that in my report, why should I?" I asked. "I was talking about Ethan, remember?"

Ethan Allen had a brother named Ira? With land to give away? I must have dozed off when I came to that part.

"But I did the report once," I told my mother the next day when she thought to ask me how things had gone with the oral report and the whole story came out. "I shouldn't have to do it again. It's not fair."

"The teacher said you have to do it?" Mom asked as she skimmed off cream for butter from the pans of milk she'd brought up from the cellar. "Then you have to do it."

"Mrs. Ford wouldn't make me," I argued while I was starting the dishes after supper was finished. "She'd give me an F, and I'd be done. She'd never have made me work another week on another report."

"Then this is your chance, bébé," Dad said.

"My chance for what?"

"Your chance to show everyone how smart you are," Dad explained as if it was obvious. Which it wasn't.

"We know how smart she is—not smart enough to do this report." Marcel laughed.

"That's right. I'm not. Besides, I don't know any more to *put* in another report," I objected. "I've got nothing to say."

"I brought you to the library last week," Mom said. "What were you doing there all that time?"

"I was reading about Ethan Allen," I replied, offended she would ask. And looking for *Unexplainable Tales, Volume II.* And hunting through dictionaries for dirty words. I don't go to the library all that often. I have a lot of things I need to do when I get there. I can't spend all my time doing schoolwork.

"Roland, you'll have to take her to the library tonight," Mom told Dad.

"Me? Why me?" Dad objected.

"I'm going over to Simone's after supper. She's perming my hair."

Marcel laughed and Dad groaned. Aunt Simone's home permanents are famous for never coming out the way they look on the box.

"I've had a hard day of work. A man shouldn't have to go nowhere after a hard day of work," Dad said.

"I shouldn't have to, either," I agreed.

"Roland . . ."

"But it's Tuesday," Dad argued. "I've got to watch TV, me. *McHale's Navy* is on Tuesdays."

"You'll be home long before that starts," Mom insisted.

"That's for sure," I said.

"I'd better be. You!" Dad ordered, pointing at Marcel. "Help your sister with the dishes so we can get out of here."

"I shouldn't have to do dishes!" Marcel yelped as our father left the kitchen for the living room and the TV. "I worked in the barn!"

"I worked in the barn, too," I said.

"I worked more."

"So what? Is it my fault I have to go to the library? No, it is not," I told him in case he couldn't figure it out on his own.

Marcel picked up a dish towel that was already too wet to use and dragged it across a pot in the dish rack.

"You know the real reason Dad doesn't want to go to the library?" he asked in a low voice after Mom went out the back door and headed for the car.

"It's because he never wants to do anything at night but watch TV. Neither do you," I pointed out as he put a plate dripping water away in the cupboard.

"That's not it," he whispered. "The real reason is . . . da old man, he can't read, him, eh?"

Marcel and I can't speak a word of French, but Marcel likes to pretend. When we were little he would go up to people and say things like, "Bishbe de loo and Pépé Lepew," trying to sound like our father and grandfather. Once he tried to say, "Hello, Uncle," by saying, "Bone shur, manure," instead of *"Bonjour, mon oncle."* He didn't make that mistake again, though he still thinks he's the master of accents. He's not.

"Talk less, work more," I suggested.

"Have you ever seen him read a book? A newspaper? A road sign?" Marcel whispered.

I didn't respond.

Marcel shrugged. "It's because he can't. He can't write, and he can't read, either. Hmmm. I wonder if he can multiply and divide?"

I didn't respond some more.

"Or add and subtract, for that matter?" Marcel continued.

I didn't respond awhile longer.

"Maybe he can't even count," Marcel suggested.

I'm ashamed to say I broke. "Of course he can count. He went to school. He can read and write, too. Probably."

"He only went to grade school. And he didn't even finish that. Tess, our father was a *grade-school dropout*." Marcel's eyes were bright, his mouth gaping in a big grin.

I had always known that. It was no secret. But there's knowing and then there's knowing.

"That doesn't mean he can't read and write, you moron," I said, mostly just to keep up my end of the conversation. My heart wasn't really in it because I had to admit that what Marcel was saying . . . well, it was possible.

By the time Dad came out to the kitchen and told me to get my coat, I was leaning against the sink, stunned by the knowledge that no matter how embarrassing a family is there are always ways they can be worse.

"It's getting late," he explained. "Let's get going."

He can tell time, I told myself as I followed him out to the truck. He knows it's getting late.

Or maybe he had just memorized the TV schedule. I told time like that until I was in third grade.

Dad never has much to say when we get started on a trip because he's always on the lookout for Brownie along both sides of the road. He has a plan to accidentally hit the dog with the truck. But Brownie always seems to know when Dad's watching for him, and, as usual, he made himself scarce.

After we were out of Brownie's territory, something

made Dad think of the seasickness story. It was probably because he'd been talking about *McHale's Navy*. Of course, anything Dad thinks of he has to talk about. That's why I had to hear—once again—about how when he was in the army air corps he was being moved somewhere on a ship and was the only man there who wasn't puking his guts out from seasickness at supper time.

"So one of those big fancy officers, who usually didn't even know us little guys were in the same room, sees me loading up my tray—I was hungry, me—and he says to me, 'With a belly like yours, why aren't you in the navy?' "

It's supposed to be funny.

Dad smiled at me and said, "I think maybe that was one of the times when I wasn't a sergeant."

Dad likes to say that he made sergeant several times while he was in the air corps. He never likes to say why he kept getting knocked back down to corporal.

Geez, I thought as Dad parked the truck next to the library. Could it be because they found out you couldn't read?

"Do . . . do you have a library card?" I asked after Dad turned off the engine.

"Hah!"

I took that to mean no.

"I always use Mom's card," I said.

"Jeannette has a library card?" Dad asked in astonishment. "What does she do with it?"

"She gets books for me."

I jumped out of the truck, slammed the door, and stomped into the library. I came back in a few minutes and pounded on the truck window. It rolled down, releasing a cloud of smoke.

"You have to come in and sign a paper so I can get my own library card," I explained.

Dad sighed as he got out of the truck. He puffed away on his cigarette until I had my hand on the handle of the door into the library. Then he carefully balanced what was left of it on the concrete border around a flower bed, hoping that he wouldn't be long and could pick up where he left off when he got back outside.

We were in the library, the only people in the area by the librarian's desk, when a horrible thought came to me.

What if Dad couldn't write his name? Ah, they had to have taught him to write his name when he was in school, I told myself.

But had I actually ever seen him do it?

The librarian handed my father a pencil and a form.

"I hate filling these things out, me," he grumbled.

Of course he would, I realized as I grabbed the form and the pencil away from him and headed over to a table where I sat down and went to work.

"Are you here to look for more information on Ethan Allen?" a sympathetic voice asked.

I jumped and turned around. There was Deborah Churchill hugging a big book against her chest and smiling down at me.

She pointed her thumb over her shoulder at a man

standing behind her. "My dad," she said, sounding as pleased as if she were introducing me to one of the Beatles.

I looked up and up until I was looking over the top of a suit (a real one, with pants and jacket that matched) at the best-looking grown-up man I'd ever seen in real life. He had dark wavy hair parted a little to one side and long dark lashes over eyes that looked out through brown-framed round glasses. His cheeks and chin were smooth—and I mean really smooth, as if he shaved every day and not just on weekends the way my father did.

I sat staring at him with my mouth open until he held out one of his soft white hands and said, "Andrew Churchill," in a low smooth voice that, if my eyes had been closed, I would have sworn was coming from a TV.

Out of the corner of my eye I saw one of my father's scaly red hands coming around me toward Mr. Churchill's. I looked at it in horror. I hoped it was clean.

As they shook hands, Dad said, "Roland LeClerc." He didn't quite pronounce the last sounds in either word. There was no way I could ever imagine that voice coming out of a TV.

"So, this is the young woman who told the class about Ethan Allen's grave being robbed," Mr. Churchill said as he looked down at me. He didn't actually smile, but it was close enough, and his eyes seemed interested. "A unique story for a sixth-grade class."

Dad dropped a hand on my shoulder. "She knows a good story when she hears one, my Thérèse."

Mr. Churchill nodded and smiled at Dad. Then he said

to him, "Deborah says you're a farmer, Mr. LeClerc. Do you keep horses?"

Dad shook his head. "Can't milk a horse."

Mr. Churchill nodded again. "I keep hearing that. Deborah, here, would like a horse, and we're trying to find a place to board one. Do you know of anyone?"

Dad rumbled around a bit while he thought. "Not too many farmers want to waste time on a horse. They don't make you no money, them."

"I keep hearing that, too. Well, it was nice meeting you. It's a school night, and I need to get Deborah home."

They turned to go over to the librarian's desk so they could check out their books. Mr. Churchill had a stack of them.

Dad bent over and put his mouth near my ear. " 'Unique,' " he whispered, repeating what Deborah's father had said about my grave-robbing story. "That's a ten-dollar word, eh?"

I rushed to complete the library form and shoved it at him. "Here," I said quietly. "I put an X on the line where you have to sign. That's all you have to do."

"Well, *merci beaucoup*," he replied in a voice you could hear all over the place.

It looks like "Roland E. LeClerc" to me, I thought as I carried the form back to the librarian. It was in cursive, too. Not very good cursive, of course. Really terrible, in fact.

Adoption was no longer enough to explain my miserable situation, I realized as I headed off to pick out a couple of "inappropriate" Ethan Allen books from their place on the shelf. I had to have been kidnapped. From a really terrific family. One of the kinds where the dads read books and wore suits and looked as if they came out of a book or a movie or some other place where the really best dads existed.

FIVE

"**W**hat do you mean, Junior Thibodeau probably can't fix my tractor?" Dad asked as he hunted for a beer in the fridge after supper the next Friday night, the night of Peggy's birthday party, the night I was spending scraping off bits of baked-on chicken skin from a cookie sheet.

"He fixes plane engines, not tractors," I explained quickly. I had the radio on, and I didn't want a lengthy conversation drowning out the sound so I would miss the program I was waiting for. "And he only does that one weekend a month when he does his National Guard duty."

"It can't be that different. If Junior can fix the National Guard's planes, he can fix my John Deere. You know, I should be in the guard, me. And Paul Thibodeau, too. Paul, he's getting a snowplow for the front of his truck. And I've got my tractor. If those Viet Cong guerrillas come over the mountains, Paul and me, we'll be ready for them. . . ."

Oh, how I wished he'd go in the other room to watch *The Wild, Wild West* and *Hogan's Heroes* like he always did on Friday nights! All his stupid talk was distracting me.

"We'll run over those big hairy monkeys," Dad announced gleefully.

I dropped the cookie sheet I'd been scrubbing into the sink filled with dirty water. "Guerrillas, not gorillas!" I cried. "They're people who fight . . . different . . . not like regular soldiers. They're not apes!"

Dad cocked his head at me and grinned. "No! You sure?" he asked.

"It was in our *Weekly Reader*."

I shook my head and groaned. You could be certain Mr. Churchill wouldn't make a mistake like that.

Then Dad suddenly threw his head back and laughed. "Paul, he told me a story this morning when I left his milk cans. As soon as he started to tell it, I thought, This is going to be a good one. Listen to this . . . There was this Communist named Rudolf, and he's having a fight with his wife. They're fighting about the weather. He says it's raining; she says it's snowing. It's raining, it's snowing, it's raining, it's snowing. They go back and forth like that for a while, them. Finally, he gets mad and he says, 'Look! Rudolf the Red knows rain, dear.'"

Dad laughed so hard Marcel came out of the living room to see what was going on. So, of course, Dad told the joke again.

"Get it?" Dad asked me while Marcel guffawed. "Rudolf the Red-Nosed Reindeer? And Communists— those people who think I shouldn't own anything, me— are called Reds. So . . ."

"Yes! Yes, I get it!" I said impatiently as I waved him

away and headed closer to the radio. "They're reading the news, so it's six o'clock. There's something I want to listen to on another station."

When I got to the radio I started madly turning the dial, hunting for accordion music. It wasn't hard to find. For some mysterious reason, the program I was looking for is one of the few that always comes in loud and clear at our house.

"*The Polka Hour!*" Marcel screeched. "You want to listen to *The Polka Hour?*"

"Yeah," I said. "You wantta make something of it? You wantta . . . polka?"

Dad banged his beer can onto the table. "I feel like a polka," he announced, and suddenly he was standing in front of me, his hands on each side of my waist, dipping in time to the music to sort of get himself going before he started spinning us through the kitchen. I grabbed his shoulders, gritted my teeth, and hung on.

" 'In heaven they have no beer . . .' " he sang along with the radio and whirled and tilted us around the table. Without pausing, he let out three whoops that, while I wouldn't want anyone I know to hear them, I have to admit were just as good as the ones Mr. Pokornowski made at the street dance last summer. Dad does know how to polka. It's just that of all the things there are in the world for a father to know how to do, dancing the polka was not the one I would have chosen for my dad's big skill.

I pulled away from him as soon as the music stopped

and leaned over the kitchen counter, my head close to the radio.

"Am I hearing what I think I'm hearing?" Mom asked as she came into the kitchen with a basket of clothes she'd just taken off the line out back. "Are you listening to *The Polka Hour*?"

"Since when have you been so interested in that?" Marcel demanded.

"Since when have you been so interested in what I'm interested in?" I replied. Then I said, "Oh, Mom, listen! It's your favorite part—the birthday announcements!"

"And birthday wishes go out to 'Nona from her favorite little boy. I'm sending you a kiss in my dreams today,' " we heard a man say.

People are always sending kisses on *The Polka Hour*'s birthday announcements. It's gross.

"And a happy sixty-seventh to 'Baby Al from the big sister who used to change your diapers,' " the man read. "A happy eighty-seventh birthday to 'Ethel Kosalski, the queen of my heart.' Stella, 'as beautiful now as you were when I first saw you four years ago,' is forty-eight. Happy birthday to Wild Bill. He's fifty-nine and wilder than ever according to 'Crazy Eddie.' "

"We'll have to send Aunt Joséphine's name in to this show for her birthday," Mom said. "She always listens."

"Shhh," I ordered.

" 'The boys at the shop' want to wish a happy birthday to 'Christine in the office.' They say they have a special

---

present for her. Little Peggy Blair is twelve years old this very night. Her 'secret admirer' says Peggy will be sure to be listening to this program during her party because she 'listens every Friday night.' Ninety-seven! That's how old Milly Coutu is. Best wishes from her great-great-grandchildren. And . . ."

I turned off the radio and turned around, trying to look innocent.

"That Blair girl listens to *The Polka Hour* every Friday night?" Mom repeated in amazement.

"She has any kind of admirer, even a secret one?" Marcel laughed.

Dad just picked up his can of beer and grinned at me.

Ah, yes, I thought, feeling warm and good all over. Bad people get punished. And Peggy is bad.

"Out of here, you!" my father shouted when I went down to the barn the next morning. "You want the sisters to think you smell of barn?"

Dad couldn't care less what the sisters who teach our catechism classes think, but he really, really doesn't like kids to smell of barn. How he can tell is beyond me, since he reeks of barn and cigarettes himself. You'd think he wouldn't be able to smell anyone else. I don't ever point that out to him, because his fear of my smelling of grain or silage or cows or something worse is what keeps me from having to do chores every morning the way I have to do them every afternoon. Marcel works down there early on Saturdays now that he's too old for religion classes, but otherwise Dad handles the morning work on his own before he makes his milk run. And that's just the way I like it.

I was sitting in the cab of the truck reading comic books when Dad climbed in. He had to get himself a cigarette before we could get started. He uses those soft packs that don't have a lid, and he likes to shake the package by snapping his wrist so a cigarette pops up by itself and he can just pull it out with his mouth. My father thinks that's sharp, I guess. Except sometimes the package is too full and the cigarettes are packed so tightly nothing comes out, and sometimes the package is too empty and the cigarettes are so loose everything comes out and goes flying all over the place. Which was what happened that morning. He ended up scrounging around on the floor of the truck for his cigarette.

Yeah. Very sharp, Dad.

It should take fifteen minutes to get to the Catholic school where the nuns teach public school kids catechism classes on Saturday mornings. But we're on the road a full hour because Dad has to make stops to pick up milk. All the farmers have it stored chilled in heavy cans with lids like mushroom caps. Each farm has a number assigned to it by the milk company and all the farmers have their number painted on the lids of their cans. When I was little, I used to like to climb up on the back of the truck and look at all the numbers and see who had the most cans, what color paint they'd used to write the numbers, who had the best penmanship. It's embarrassing how little it took to amuse me back then.

Once Dad realized he wasn't going to get a chance to chase Brownie up and down the road with a truck partially loaded with eight or ten milk cans banging all over the place, he started talking about how funny *Hogan's Heroes* had been the night before. I had liked it, too. It was one of those stories where Colonel Hogan sneaks out of the German prisoner-of-war camp he's stuck in during World War II. He just leaves for a while so he can do some spying in town for the American and British military groups he and his followers secretly work for. I always like those stories because they show that Hogan could have left for a safer place whenever he wanted to. He just stayed because fighting the Nazis was more important than getting away.

"Mrs. Ford doesn't like *Hogan's Heroes*," I told Dad.

"No! How can she not like Hogan, her? He makes me laugh the whole show long. He's a tricky one."

"Mrs. Ford says war isn't funny. She says it isn't right to make jokes about prisoner-of-war camps because they weren't funny places and people didn't have good times in them. Mrs. Ford says *Hogan's Heroes* is in bad taste," I explained.

"Oh, bad taste." Dad made a rude noise to let me know what he thought of bad taste. Oddly enough, rude noises are a good example of something Mrs. Ford thinks is in bad taste.

"I don't laugh when the good guys have to eat watery soup or have no fingers on their gloves. That's not funny. I laugh when Hogan, he makes fun of the bad guys. It's good to laugh at the big bad guys. It makes it harder for them to be bad to the little good guys. It makes things fairer. That's just common sense."

Dad tapped the steering wheel with the two fingers that gripped what was left of his lit cigarette as spoke. He may have been trying to make sure he got his point across. Or he may have just been trying to wave his hands and drive at the same time. He always waves his hands when he talks, sending ashes, food, whatever he's holding flying all over the place.

"Ask Mrs. Ford what she did in the war. I don't remember seeing her when I was in it. And if I want to laugh at *Hogan's Heroes*, me, I'm going to laugh at *Hogan's Heroes*. I don't need any teacher telling me what to think."

We finally drove into town and were stopped at an intersection when I looked up to see a line of dark green-and-brown trucks passing in front of us.

"Look!" Dad shouted. "There's Junior!"

Dad started blowing his horn and Junior Thibodeau, riding in the back of the fourth truck marked "Vermont Air National Guard, the Green Mountain Boys," answered by jumping to his feet, pulling off his cap, and waving it while roaring, "Hey, Rolie!" He was a big rubbery guy like his brother, Jack, and all the other Thibodeau kids. It was quite a sight.

I sank down below the truck's windows while Dad laughed and said, "That Junior, he's something, eh?"

He's just your godson, I thought as I cringed out of sight. He's not even a blood relative. What would you do if you saw Marcel in the back of a truck?

Please, God, I prayed. Don't let me be there when that happens.

We pulled up in front of the Catholic school. Before I could escape out of the truck door, Dad grabbed my arm. "I didn't mean you shouldn't listen to Mrs. Ford just because she doesn't know a good TV show when she sees one. Mrs. Ford, she's a good woman. Remember that."

"A good woman." That's what my father calls any woman he has to say something nice about when nothing nice comes immediately to mind. "A good woman" is a woman who's good but you wish she wasn't.

For instance, the nuns are good women. Especially ol' Sister Marie Hélène, who went to her reward long before I was born, though her memory lingers on. Her main claim to fame at our house is that she made Dad learn the Act of Contrition two years before everyone else in his catechism class because she said any prayer that included the words "I am heartily sorry" was one he was going to be saying a lot.

"Now, I know that Sister Marie Hélène had to know her Act of Contrition in French. Her accent was as heavy as my mother's." (That is an important part of the story that Dad insists on including whenever he tells the tale.) "But that good woman, she thought she was being so clever by making everybody learn it in English. I fixed her! I didn't understand a word, me!"

I don't think he knows what "contrite" or "contrition" means to this day. My father is not someone who ever seems sorry for much that he's done. He certainly never sounds apologetic for the fact that when he was a kid he didn't memorize those questions and answers that are almost all you do, along with some lengthy praying, in catechism class. When he was told that the answer to "Why did God make me?" was "So I could be happy with Him in Heaven," he said to his teacher, "I sure hope so. I'm not too happy right here, me."

I think that easily explains why so many of the good women at the Catholic school remembered him when Marcel and I got to them, for which I "am heartily sorry."

Peggy, of course, had all the makings of a good woman. You could always depend on her to be at catechism class. She always got saints' cards at the end of the year for perfect attendance, and she kept them, too, unlike a lot of the other kids who traded them for gum (they weren't worth a chocolate bar) or lost them before they got home. So, of course she was there when I climbed out of the truck and started across the paved Catholic school playground looking as if I didn't have anything on my mind at all.

She and Yvette Morrissette were standing under the basketball hoop, moaning and groaning about how tired they were from the party the night before.

"Hey, Pokie," I said when I came across him a little distance away. "Were you guys listening to *The Polka Hour* last night?"

"We weren't home."

"I was listening," a girl said. She started shouting and walking toward Peggy. "Hey, Peggy! You were on the radio last night!"

"I was?" Peggy replied, looking a lot less tired.

"Yeah! They read your name during the birthday announcements on *The Polka Hour.*"

The smile on Peggy's face couldn't have left any more rapidly if it had been washed off with a great big rag. Her chin dropped and her eyes started to pop.

"I heard it, too," someone said.

"Me, too," I called.

A circle was starting to form around Peggy and Yvette as word of Peggy's fame spread around the yard. She looked from one of us to another, horrified.

"You . . . you . . . listen to *The Polka Hour?*" she stammered. "I didn't think anyone under a hundred listened to that."

"Why, Peggy, the announcer said you were going to be listening to the program during your birthday party," I said sweetly. "Did you guys have a good time?"

Yvette stepped back from Peggy. "I do *not* listen to *The Polka Hour.* Nobody listens to that."

"I don't listen, either," Peggy squealed. She turned to Yvette. "Tell them. I only listen to WKBW. They don't play polkas on that station."

"I wasn't listening to *The Polka Hour,* either," the girl who had told Peggy about the announcement said. "It was my mother. She was listening, and she told me."

I lowered my head so no one could see me smiling. There's no better feeling than to have a plan work out the way it's supposed to. It wasn't exactly revenge, which some people think is wrong though I have no problem with it, myself. It was more like . . . justice. It was more like fair play. Finally.

"Come on, Peggy," one of the boys jeered. "You listen to *The Polka Hour* every week. The announcer said so."

"And how would he know?"

"Why, Peggy," I said. "The announcer knows you listen to *The Polka Hour* every Friday night because your secret admirer told him so."

As soon as I heard the sound of my own voice I knew I'd missed another one of those opportunities to keep my mouth shut. But once you realize something like that, it's too late. Way too late.

Time stopped for an instant. Peggy's head snapped up, her body went rigid, and she stood totally still for a second. Then she repeated, "My 'secret admirer'?" as a big smile spread across her face.

Everyone started talking at once, explaining to Peggy that her secret admirer had called in her birthday announcement, answering her questions, and repeating every word about her they could remember from the radio program. Then Peggy, Yvette, and a couple of other girls started carrying on about Peggy and her new, unknown boyfriend.

While I stood to one side muttering a word for the stuff in the barn my father is afraid I'll smell of.

SIX

*O*n the next Monday, before lunch, three weeks after Mr. Santangelo's arrival, I gave my oral report again. But first I had to listen to talk of Peggy's secret admirer while I was riding the bus to school. And before class started. And during morning recess.

I was in a really bad mood.

" 'Ethan Allen was born in Connecticut,' " I began when I got up in the middle of our circle of desks and started reading. I didn't say he was born in 1738 because I never remember dates so I figured no one else would either. " 'Which makes a person wonder why someone in Vermont has to do a report on him.

"He was the oldest of eight kids. His parents were considered oddballs. They believed that God allowed people to make decisions for themselves without planning out every minute of their lives for them, which was what most people back then believed. Predestination, they called it. From the time you were born everything that was going to happen to you was already planned,

---

80

in other words predestined. You couldn't change it. That was before the population explosion we're always hearing about so it was probably easier to believe then that God had time to plan everyone's life for them.

"Ethan liked to argue about religion, which annoyed the neighbors, and who can blame them? It also made his parents think he was smart and ought to go to college so he could become successful and help out the rest of the family. They sent him to study with a cousin who was a minister so Ethan could go to Yale, that being where everyone went to school back then. You can guess what happened."

"No, we can't," Pokie broke in.

"Come on, you guys," I complained when everyone agreed with him. "What always happened in the old days when the eldest son was preparing to go to college? Haven't any of you ever read a book? The father died! When Ethan was seventeen his father died, and he had to quit studying so he could support his mother and his seven younger brothers and sisters. He was a dropout."

It was right about that point that I got tired of writing while I was preparing the report. I jumped a whole bunch of stuff and tried to hurry things up. There's no point in drawing out these kinds of things too long.

"Years pass. Many years. Ethan goes from job to job and spends a lot of time drinking in taverns, swearing, and making church leaders mad. Then he ends up in Vermont, which wasn't Vermont then, it was something else. There was a land dispute that you wouldn't understand. Some more years pass. War breaks out. Ethan walks into Fort Ticonderoga one morning with the Green Mountain Boys while most of the British soldiers are still asleep, takes it over, and drinks the British commander's rum. A while later he's captured by the British near Montreal. He's held captive for almost three years. He goes home. The American leaders don't want to let Vermont join the union because they think the new country should only be for the original thirteen colonies, the people there being educated and classy, which the people in Vermont are not. Ethan and his buddies say, 'Nuts to you'—sort of—and declare Vermont an independent republic. The American leaders change their minds and let Vermont become the fourteenth state. Ethan has some kind of attack on his way home from buying hay and dies. The end."

I dropped down into my chair with a plop.

"That's *it*?" Jack asked.

"I hit all the high points," I told him.

"I expected it to be more interesting," Wayne said.

"It was interesting when I did it last week, and I was told I had to do it over!" I complained. "I wasn't going to make that mistake again."

"I never said you shouldn't be interesting, Thérèse—though it would be nice if you were interesting in less . . . interesting . . . ways. I believe what I said was that you should have your facts in order and not skip around in time," Mr. Santangelo reminded me.

I threw my hands up in the air. "The guy was born at the beginning of the report, and he died at the end. I did my job."

"You started it."

I didn't like the sound of that. "I did it . . . twice."

"But you didn't explain why Ethan Allen is important to us," Mr. Santangelo said.

"That's because he isn't important to us."

"If he wasn't important, people wouldn't always be talking about him and the Green Mountain Boys," Peggy broke in.

"Who were the Green Mountain Boys?" Pokie asked.

I gave him a kick and said, "Sh."

"Thérèse, do you see what you've done wrong?" Mr. Santangelo asked.

"No."

He gave this big sigh, like I was ruining his life or something when it was the other way around.

"Maybe it would help if you gave us some details about some of the things you mentioned in your report," he suggested, though he didn't sound as if it was very likely.

"Yeah, tell us about Ethan taking Fort Ti," Wayne ordered.

"Tell us about his drinking and swearing!" Jack exclaimed.

"Okay," I agreed. "Once—"

"No, no, no," Mr. Santangelo broke in. "Tell us about something else. Anything else."

"Ah, geez." I slouched down at my desk, running over in my mind everything I'd read. "Well, let me think. I could tell you . . . no, that's no good. Or there's the story . . . no, I can't remember how that ends. Oh, I'll try this one.

"While Ethan was still living in Connecticut," I began without standing up again because I thought I'd done enough standing up in front of everybody for one day, "he had this friend. Thomas something, his name was. They used to read a lot."

Jack snorted. "That sounds like fun."

"Wait until you hear what they read—stuff about how there are laws that aren't laws, but they're still laws and people know these laws, even if they haven't been written down by someone important. In fact, these laws probably haven't been written down at all. Everyone's just supposed to figure them out using reason or something."

Pokie's hand shot up in the air and he started going, "Oh! Oh! I know what those laws are!"

"No, you *don't*."

"Yes, I do. Let me say."

"You *don't*, Pokie!"

"Yes, I do! Yes, I do! It's like when you do something that no one has ever actually told you not to do, but your parents chew you out for it anyway and say you shouldn't have done it because, 'Yoooou know the difference between right and wrong.' "

"Oh. Well. Maybe that's it," I said uncertainly.

"And then when you say, 'Everyone else was doing it,' your parents say, 'Yoooou know the difference between right and wrong even if all your friends don't,' " Pokie continued.

"Okay, okay," I said, trying to shut him up. I was the one who had been asked to keep talking, after all. "So they read these books that said there were laws about right and wrong that anyone with common sense could figure out, and that what's right is right even if kings and those sorts say it's not. These books said that if your government broke those laws about right and wrong you should rebel against it. These books said that one of the laws stated that no one should take the life, liberty, or property of another."

"Excellent, Thérèse, excellent. This is exactly the kind of thing you should be putting in an oral report," Mr. Santangelo said, sounding a little perkier than he had been.

That may have been true, but the rest of the class was beginning to start watching the clock. Fortunately, I had saved the good stuff for last.

"They also read about smallpox," I said, leaning forward and lowering my voice as if I was telling them something really juicy. "It's like chicken pox, only worse. You start out with a fever and muscle aches and maybe some puking. Then you get a rash. Then the rash turns into pus-filled pimples. Then the pus-filled pimples might get infected. If you're lucky, you're just left with great big scars. If you're not . . ."

I ran a finger across my throat and made a cutting sound.

"There was a disease like that on *Dr. Kildare* last week!" Peggy exclaimed.

I find *Dr. Kildare* a little dull myself. It would be a much better show if there was less talking and more operations and incurable diseases. But Dr. Kildare is played by this really good-looking guy, so Peggy and her friends love it.

"Well, smallpox was a much bigger problem back in Ethan's time than it is wherever Dr. Kildare lives. In Europe there was smallpox going around all the time. A lot of grown-ups became immune to it because they had it when they were kids. But over here smallpox wasn't as common. The Indians had never even heard of it before they started catching it from the white people who brought it over here. No one was immune."

I said "No one . . . was immune" with a little pause and looked very serious the way Dr. Kildare might if he told someone, "I'm sorry . . . there's no cure. In six months you will . . . have grown another head."

"Why are you telling us about this when you're supposed to be telling us about Ethan Allen?" Wayne asked, which sort of spoiled the effect I was trying to create.

"Because Ethan and his friend . . . Did I mention that he was a doctor? Well, he was . . . they had read about inoculating people for smallpox. Someone had figured out that if you intentionally put some live smallpox into healthy people, they'd get the disease, but it wasn't as bad so they had a better chance of living. Sometimes towns would start inoculating people if they thought an epidemic was coming. But—"

"How did they inoculate people back then? Did they have needles?" Yvette broke in.

"I don't know! Maybe they cut people open and shoved smallpox pus into them. It doesn't matter. What was I going to say? Oh, yeah, it was against the law to inoculate anyone without a town leader's permission. And one of the reasons it was against the law was that a lot of the ministers back then were against it. They thought you should rely on God to save you, not man-made science.

"So Ethan, who didn't like ministers, anyway, because he thought they used the Bible to give themselves power over other people, and his friend decide this is a foolish law and people should be able to save themselves. It seems like common sense. So they rebel against their town. Thomas inoculates Ethan for smallpox—without permission. On a Sunday. In front of a church."

"What did Ethan Allen look like?" someone asked.

"Would you guys stop it with the interruptions? I don't care what he looked like!"

As I was saying (well, shouting) those words I was looking right into Deborah's shocked face. I had shouted at Deborah.

"He's supposed to have been big," I said quickly, in my very nicest voice. "The books all say he was very big and very strong."

I took a deep breath and continued. "There they are, on a Sunday, in front of the church, breaking the law. And, of course, a minister who also happens to have been one of the selectmen comes along. As luck would have it, he's

Ethan's cousin, which you'd think would be a good thing. Evidently it wasn't, because after going back and forth about it for a while Ethan ends up shouting, 'By Jesus Christ, I wish I may be bound down in hell with—' "

"Thérèse! Thérèse!" Mr. Santangelo broke in. "Cool it!"

"I give up! It is impossible to give a report here."

"You can't use that kind of language in a classroom," Mr. Santangelo explained in a high, excited voice.

"But it's a quote."

"Well . . . well . . ." Mr. Santangelo sputtered.

"Ethan had to go to court for talking like that. It was against the law back then," I explained. "And he found some loose pigs in his garden, locked them up in a pen, and had to go to court because he was supposed to lock them up in some special pig pound. And he ripped his clothes off and started beating somebody up—actually, two some-bodies—and he had to go to court for that. And . . ."

"How did he *ever* become a famous hero?" Deborah asked.

"I told you not to talk about his bad language," Mr. Santangelo reminded me.

"I wasn't. I was talking about how he didn't get along with church leaders. And he didn't get along with the guy whose pigs he locked up. And he didn't get along with those people he beat up. And that, class, is what you should know about Ethan Allen—he didn't get along. The end. Again.

"You know, Mr. Santangelo," I said, without giving him

time to give my last talk much thought, "I really gave almost two reports today and counting the one last week that's three. I was thinking maybe I should get a B."

Mr. Santangelo had been known to ask us what we thought we'd earned for a grade, so I figured it wouldn't hurt to make a suggestion.

"But everyone else did oral reports that had something to do with the state of Vermont," Peggy complained. "She didn't tell us very much about Vermont."

She should have been grateful. The state of Vermont isn't my idea of a fascinating subject.

"Make her do it again. But this time make her put in more stuff about Ethan taking his clothes off and fighting," Jack ordered. "And more bad language. I might actually read a book once in a while if I could find one with bad language."

"Peggy has a point, Thérèse. These oral reports are supposed to be about the state of Vermont. Tell us about Ethan in Vermont, and I'll give you a B. But the oral report has got to be finished."

"It *is* finished," I pointed out. "I'm not doing any more."

"Ethan is still in Connecticut. Finish the report, and you can have a B."

"Well, then, just give me a D," I said.

Mr. Santangelo shook his head. "I think that since Ethan Allen was the topic that everyone wanted, you should have to complete it. You have to keep working until you've earned your B.

"And this Fort Ticonderoga that Wayne keeps mentioning—I've heard it might be a good place for a field trip," he concluded.

I sat at my seat with my mouth open while everyone around me carried on about how great it would be to go somewhere where we might see someone who was still alive. I couldn't believe it. I was actually beginning to miss Mrs. Ford.

• • •

So, after having worked for two weeks and standing before my classmates on two separate Mondays, I still had to give an oral report on Ethan Allen. Not that I really worked a week each on those reports. Not even close. That's not my point. My point is that the oral report was always there.

It was like when you're trapped in that dream. I don't mean the one where you're at school, look down at yourself, and realize that you're wearing a pair of goofy pajamas (maybe unbuttoned, too) and that it's only a matter of time before everyone else notices. I mean the other one, the one where you have to do something (dial the phone so you can call for help, open a door so you can get away from something) and no matter how hard you try you just can't finish what it is you have to do.

Even though I wasn't trying all that hard, the not finishing part was the same.

What made things a whole lot worse was that there was some muttering in the classroom about my being given too many chances. Sometimes I overheard suggestions that I ought to just fail and get it over with. Sometimes people said it straight out, right to my face. These were, of course, the people with easy oral report topics that involved poster boards full of pictures. The report on dairy farming—it must have taken Yvette a good twenty minutes to throw that together. She didn't even get her pictures from magazines. She used snapshots of herself standing next to cows in her father's barn. Lynn Smid's pictures came out of the Vermont Marble Company's annual report. Her father works there, for crying out loud. And I don't know why Peggy got so upset about not getting Ethan Allen for her oral report topic. Her report on the University of Vermont had to be ten or twenty times easier to do than mine. She had dozens of pictures of the college—every picture you could ever imagine of buildings, teachers, and students was pasted up on her *three* sheets of poster board.

"I had hundreds of pictures to choose from," she told me afterward in that whiney voice of hers that made it sound as if she'd just suffered through something awful. "Maybe thousands."

Deborah had the best report of all—gravestone rubbings. What that had to do with Vermont I don't know, but wouldn't it just figure that Deborah would be able to get whatever topic she wanted.

I never even really wanted any particular topic. I just got stuck with Ethan Allen. If it hadn't been for all his swearing and fighting, I don't know how I would have been able to stand it.

At least I wouldn't have to stand it for much longer. Mr. Santangelo told me I was going to have to pick up the pace. Instead of giving me a week to do my oral report over, I only had two nights.

SEVEN

" 'The gods of the hills are not the gods of the valleys,' " I said in a low voice as I shoveled last year's silage out of the silo at one end of our barn and into a wheelbarrow. The tall, cylinder-shaped silo was almost empty so I could walk right in it without worrying about being smothered in tons of sharp-smelling chopped cornstalks. My voice went up and up, not actually echoing but filling the big wooden tube I was standing in. There was no other place where I sounded so good.

" 'The gods of the hills are not the gods of the valleys,' " I said again, trying to sound big and manly.

"When you talk to yourself, you can always be sure of a good conversation, eh?" Dad said. He had just pulled a full milking machine out from under a cow and was stretching in the opening between the silo and the barn.

I laid a hand on my chest and raised the other up in the air. " 'The gods of the hills are not the gods of the valleys.' "

I drew out the word "not" and made my voice quiver when I said, "of the valleys."

"Bon," Dad said, nodding his head. "Good. I like that."

"Do you get it?" I asked.

"What it means? Of course. Who wouldn't?"

I wouldn't, for one. "Ah . . . good. I like the way it sounds so I'm going to use it in the oral report I have to give tomorrow."

"Another oral report?" Dad asked.

"Not exactly. You know how you kept working your way up to sergeant when you were in the air corps, and then you kept going back to corporal so you had to work your way up to sergeant again? Well, that's how it is with me and this oral report on Ethan Allen."

Evidently that wasn't a good comparison. "Have you been getting in trouble at school, you?" Dad demanded. "Fighting with the other kids? Sassing your teacher? You been talking dirty, eh?"

"I haven't done any of that stuff! Why would you think such a thing? Mr. Santangelo just keeps making me do more on that same oral report. You know, I don't think he knows how to teach, Dad. Maybe . . ."

Dad waved a hand at me as he started to turn back toward the cows waiting for him in the barn. "Don't try to trick me. If you do a job right, you don't have to do it again. Any fool knows that."

"You try reading those old Ethan Allen books, if you think 'doing the job right' is so easy!" I yelled after him.

It was not an awful thing for a kid to say to her parent, assuming her parent was able to try reading books. Other kids could say it without having to worry about more than being told they were disrespectful. But not me. I had to stand there cringing, waiting for one of those awful things to happen that you see in television shows when kids say something cruel to their folks. Once on a soap opera a mom started sobbing and ran out into the rain where she was hit by a car, and I'm always seeing shows where dads decide that the only way they can make their selfish, ungrateful families happy is to begin a life of crime. All my dad did was tell me to be quiet because I was bothering his cows. Not that I wanted him to embarrass the whole family by robbing a bank and ending up in prison, but it would be nice to think that he at least knew being uneducated is more important than whether or not his cows are being annoyed.

I went back and forth between being mad at my father for calling me a fool because I was still working on my report and being mad at myself for yelling at him about reading. By the time I sat down in my room at the old table that I use for a desk, I was just mad. I tried to remember the wise old saying about how you can't pick your relatives but you can pick your friends and you can pick your nose but you can't pick your friend's nose. Or your relative's, either. Or something like that. However it went, it was very true.

There's only one way to do the job right the first time or any time was what I should have told Dad, I decided, and that is with pictures. Which I *don't* have. No wonder they say a picture is worth a thousand words. You hold up a picture during an oral report and that's a thousand words you don't have to say or write or read.

I shoved *The Narrative of Colonel Ethan Allen's Captivity* along the top of the table and let it hit the wall. That was a book title that at least told you something. It was the story of Ethan's imprisonment by the British. If I lived long enough to get that far in my report, I would make an attempt to skim a few pages. But I had years of his life to get through before he was captured, and that meant reading more of these other two books that were both called just *Ethan Allen*. They weren't called *Ethan Allen Leaves Connecticut and Goes Somewhere Else* or *Ethan Allen Enlists in the Army*, so I could just pick them up, find what I wanted, and then go on to read something more fun like those earthquake, flood, and fire stories in *Reader's Digest*.

No, these books were like garbage cans into which somebody had dumped everything they knew about Ethan. I had already picked through them looking for the good, reusable things. Now I was going to have to dig through the icky stuff.

And it's all going to be for nothing, I thought as I propped my elbow on the table, dropped my forehead onto my hand, and started to flip one unillustrated page after another. An oral report without anything to look at is just . . . what? Words? It might as well be a stinking poem.

Poetry, of course, made me think of Mr. Santangelo. And because I was thinking of Mr. Santangelo, I thought of school, and that got me back to my oral report. And thinking about school *and* my oral report made me think of Pokie. Pokie, who I go to school with and who was to blame for my getting an oral report topic that had no pictures to go with it and who really ought to help me out since it was his fault and he thought we were getting married someday.

And then I started thinking about a way that he *could* help me out.

Pokie was all for my plan when I told him about it the next morning. That wasn't exactly a tribute to my idea . . . Pokie is all for any plan that includes him. And this one meant someone (me) would be rehearsing with him during recess and lunchtime. He'll agree to almost anything for company.

But by the time we came to actually putting the plan into action, a couple of things had happened to give him second thoughts, the main one being that Mr. Santangelo was in as bad a mood as we'd ever seen him.

After lunch he had read us that Robert Frost poem about the guy deciding what path to take in the woods. He's very big on reading us poems by Robert Frost because Frost spent a lot of time in Vermont and that is supposed to make us like poetry, though it hasn't made any difference as far as I'm concerned. He had just finished those last few lines:

> "Two roads diverged in a wood, and I—
> I took the one less traveled by,
> And that has made all the difference"

when Wayne raised his hand.

"Don't you think it's awful the way people in Vermont have so little respect for Robert Frost, Mr. Santangelo?" he asked.

Mr. Santangelo settled himself on the edge of the desk, looking all thoughtful as if he was getting ready for a long, serious talk. "What do you mean, Wayne?"

"Why, all winter long we put signs up along the sides of our roads that say Frost Heaves."

That was exactly the kind of joke you'd expect Wayne to make. It was sort of brainy, what with being about a poet and all, and not very funny. You could tell from the big grin on his face that he thought he was going to get a gold star or something for it. And he might have, if Jack hadn't started banging his desk and going, "Pukes. He said Robert Frost pukes." Then Pokie went, "Oh, I get it. Pavement heaves up because of the frost, and Robert Frost heaves, too." At that point Peggy started making this "Ha-ha, ha-ha, ha-ha!" noise, which, to her, anyway, is the sound of laughter.

One thing led to another, until Mr. Santangelo quietly stood up and said, "I love Robert Frost. Thank you for ruining this poem for me."

Which was bad enough. But then Jack made it worse by calling out, "You're welcome."

It was right about then that Mr. Santangelo said it was time for me to give my report. That is what people mean when they talk about bad timing. If your teacher is in a snit before you even open your mouth . . . well, why bother?

When I got up, the boys were still bending over and

pulling their hands away from their mouths, pretending they were barfing up streams of upchuck while the girls were groaning, pretending they didn't think it was funny. They were not exactly in the mood for an oral report, in my opinion, and evidently in Pokie's, too. I could tell by the way he was clutching the sides of his desk that he was getting stage fright. I began:

"After Ethan got into that fight I told you about, he had to go to court. While he was there . . ."

I stopped reading and gave Pokie a look. He frantically shook his head.

"While he was there . . ." I repeated while Pokie continued to shake.

"While he was there," I said one last time, pulling back my right leg as if I was getting ready to give someone a good swift kick, which finally brought Pokie up out of his chair.

". . . he ripped off his shirt again, raised his fist toward one of the men who was pressing charges against him, told him he was a liar, and threatened anyone who tried to stop him. From doing what, I don't know. Ethan wasn't actually thrown out of town because of that, but the judge did say he'd drop charges if he left."

The plan had been for Pokie to act out Ethan's actions, creating a sort of moving picture. But he was overcome with such shyness that all he did was pull his striped pullover shirt up just high enough to show off a few inches of his skinny gut, raise one hand in what looked more like a wave than a fist, and run back to his seat.

There was a stunned silence—we had finally brought the heave-ho jokes to an end—until Jack said, "What was that?"

And everyone went crazy all over again. I read out over the noise:

> "He didn't just leave town, he left Connecticut and bought a mine in Massachusetts with some of his wife's relatives."

Pokie must have felt encouraged by the response to his first act, because he jumped up and pretended to be using a hammer in a mine.

> "But that didn't work out well, so he ended up owing people money. Plus, he was still arguing about religion all the time, so he didn't make a lot of friends there."

Pokie pointed a finger and made his mouth go as if he was talking to someone.

> "That time he really did get kicked out of town."

Pokie pretended he'd just received a kick in the backside.

> "Ethan and his wife and children had to go back to Connecticut and move in with one of his brothers. It's awful to think that you might have to have your brother living with you still when you're both grown up. Personally, I'm living for the day when my brother

is old enough to go . . . anywhere. But Heman Allen had to take in Ethan, his wife, Mary, and their two kids. The kids were little, so they were probably all right, but the wife was mean. She was so mean. . . ."

"How mean was she?" Pokie asked from where he was standing next to me.

"Mary Allen was so mean that once she took after her own brothers with an ax."

"How mean was she?" Pokie asked again.

"She was so mean that once when Ethan was passing the graveyard late at night on his way home from a tavern, a bunch of boys with sheets held over their heads with brooms jumped out at him. In creepy voices they said they were devils and they were going to take him off with them to hell. Ethan just sat on his horse and said, 'Tell your master that I'm not afraid of him. I'm married to his sister!' "

"How mean was she?" the whole class shouted.

"She was so mean that when she died the gravedigger said he'd never dug a grave he enjoyed more."

"How mean . . ."
"Enough!" Mr. Santangelo called out. He jumped up from the top of Mrs. Ford's desk and took Pokie's arm. "You can go back to your desk now, Peter."
"But he's part of my report," I objected.

"That part of your report is over."

"But it was the best part," Jack said.

"He's my pictures. They all liked having him up here," I told Mr. Santangelo, waving a hand toward the rest of the class.

"I didn't," he said. "Now move things along."

He didn't have to tell me twice. I quickly skipped through the stuff about how bad it was for Ethan to have to live with his brother. Particularly since he was the oldest son and head of the family, and he was thirty years old with a wife and kids. Without Pokie clutching his head and wiping away fake tears, it didn't sound as dramatic as I wanted it to. I went right to the part about how Ethan and one of his other brothers started going north toward Canada to hunt for furs. That was how he first found out about the new towns that were growing up in the Green Mountains between New Hampshire and New York.

"The land in the Green Mountains was cheap because no one knew for certain who owned it. New Hampshire had been selling grants to it for twenty years, but all that time New York said it owned it, too. Farmers could buy small amounts of land from New Hampshire and own their own place. The New Yorkers didn't want to sell to small farmers. They wanted to divide the land up among other rich New Yorkers who wouldn't live on it themselves. They'd just rent it to people and make money that way.

"For years people had been trying to get the king of England, who ruled us then, to decide who had the right to sell the land in this place everyone called the New Hampshire Grants. Finally, he said it belonged to New York. New Yorkers started taking the farmers in the Green Mountains to court, so they could force them to leave their homes.

"Ethan, who had failed at everything he'd ever tried to do and was always getting dragged into court over something or other anyway, decided to start buying this land so he could get himself into more trouble. About the same time, a group of men who owned a chunk of land there hired Ethan to help manage it."

"Yes?" I said to Pokie, who was leaning over from the desk next to mine, trying to get my attention.

"Are there going to be more jokes?"

"No," I said.

"You need some more jokes."

"And Thérèse?" Deborah asked before I could start talking. "What about Ethan Allen's horse?"

"Did he have a horse?" I asked.

"You mentioned he was riding a horse when those boys near a cemetery tried to scare him. Did he have a favorite horse? Lots of famous soldiers did."

Then she rattled off a list of names of what I guess must be famous old dead horses that had belonged to famous old dead guys.

"The books I read never said anything about his horse," I explained.

"Are you ever going to start talking about Vermont?" Peggy complained.

"What do you think the New Hampshire Grants were?" I tried to use a tone of voice that suggested Peggy was an idiot without my having to say so. If you actually say so, you get in trouble. If you make people figure it out for themselves, you don't. "I'm talking about the land between New York and New Hampshire. What else is there *besides* Vermont."

"Yeah, Peggy, you moron," Jack, who either didn't know how to avoid getting into trouble or didn't care, said.

"Some New Yorkers were taking some farmers to court. Those farmers lived on land they'd bought from the men who hired Ethan. The New Yorkers claimed they owned the land the farmers lived on and wanted to evict them from their homes. Ethan was hired to help the farmers because if they lost the court case, other New Yorkers could evict other small farmers from their land in the Grants, too. Lots of people would lose everything they had. And since Ethan—and his brothers and cousins because Ethan talked most of his family into moving north into the Green Mountains with him—were going to end up farmers there, too, they could also lose everything they had.

"And then what would happen to them? When

Ethan got in trouble before, he went home to Connecticut and his family. Now there was no home and family in Connecticut. If New York could get control of all the land in the New Hampshire Grants, the Allens would either be thrown out of their homes with no place to go or they would have to live as tenants, supporting the rich New Yorkers who had taken over the land the Allens, themselves, had paid for.

"So the court case was important. Ethan hired a lawyer and the two of them rode up to Albany to go to court with the farmers. As soon as they got into the building, Ethan saw how things were going to end up. The New Yorkers walked into court in their fine clothes looking easy and comfortable because they were just landlords, and collecting rents doesn't take a lot of effort. Then the Grantsmen went in worn out from working the same farms the New Yorkers were trying to take away from them. They lost before a word was said.

"Ethan thought any case heard in a New York court would always benefit the New Yorkers. They owned the courts. He decided the farmers in the Grants would have to fight for their land some other way.

"But before he could get back to the Grants to start the fight, a New York lawyer offered him money and land if he'd join their side. Ethan said no, and when the lawyer asked him why, when the farmers didn't have a chance against the rich New Yorkers, Ethan said to him, 'The gods of the hills are not the gods of the valleys.' "

That was it, the big finish, the first memorable thing Ethan said—as far as I could tell—that didn't involve damning somebody. I stopped speaking and looked out across my audience. My audience looked back. The words that had bounced up and down and all around our old silo didn't do much of anything there in that classroom. I tried to fix things.

"You can see what he meant, and . . . uh . . ."

"I don't see what he meant," Pokie said.

"You never see anything," I snapped.

"I don't get it, either."

"Me, neither."

"Perhaps you'd better explain it to them, Thérèse," Mr. Santangelo suggested. He was looking at me as if I explained things all the time.

"Well, 'the gods of the hills' are . . . You know how long ago people believed in more than one god? And some people in one place believed in one group of gods and some people in another place believed in another group? He was sort of talking about that."

That sounded pretty good, I thought, and I rushed on to talk about something else, even though I really didn't have anything else to talk about.

"But why did Ethan say it to that lawyer at that time? Why did it answer the lawyer's question about why Ethan wouldn't help the New Yorkers?" Mr. Santangelo asked.

"And if Ethan Allen was such a loser and didn't have a job, why didn't he just take the money and work for the side that had the best chance of winning? It would have been the smart thing to do," Deborah said.

"It . . . it . . . ah . . . Come on, you know," I said to Mr. Santangelo, trying to get him to let me off the hook.

Mr. Santangelo sighed and sat back in his chair. "Maybe you'd better just finish up, Thérèse."

"Yeah, Tess."

"Make it fast."

"I'd rather be taking a dictation test than listening to this."

"Yeah. At least a dictation test ends."

I knew I had a good story. This guy, Ethan Allen, who couldn't seem to do anything right, was getting himself involved in this fight with rich, powerful people who could easily beat him. That was good! That was interesting! Why didn't they get it? If I just had one good picture to hold up . . . What else could I do to make them see? Or to at least keep them from laughing at me?

"Wait! Wait a minute!" I said, thinking as fast as I could. "I know it. I know what he meant. He meant . . . he meant," I repeated, hoping it would come to me. ". . . that the people who lived in the Grants—in the Green Mountains—were different from the people who lived in other places like New York—the valleys. He meant that no matter what the courts said, no matter what the New York government said, no matter what the king said, the farmers in the Grants weren't going to spend their lives working to make some landlord rich the way the New Yorkers wanted them to."

I could feel someone staring at me. It was Wayne. He was nodding his head slowly. "Joining the New York side would have been the smart thing to do, but it wouldn't have been the *right* thing," he said. "He was obeying one of those unwritten laws that he used to read about, the one about not taking the life, liberty, or property of another."

"Uh . . . yeah. That's it. You've got it," I said, wishing I'd thought of that.

"Ethan meant that you don't have to be rich to be right," Pokie added.

"*And* you don't have to be *smart* to be right," Jack broke in. I think that was a little off the point, myself, but it was easy to understand why Jack would like to think it was true even though, in his case, it rarely was.

Suddenly, things were looking better. That was good since I was going to have to quit for the day, and I didn't want to leave anybody in a bad mood.

"It's funny the way Ethan was always fighting and then ended up in the middle of a fight he didn't get started himself. It's almost as if something had drawn him up there to the Green Mountains," I said as I sat down.

I just made that part up on the spur of the moment. I liked it because it sounded like something out of *Unexplainable Tales.*

"That was much better, Thérèse, but it's still not finished," Mr. Santangelo pointed out. "Is it?"

"There was too much left to do in one night, Mr. Santangelo. No one could have finished it."

There was a pause as if everyone figured Peggy was

going to say, "*I* could have," anyway, so we might as well take a breath so she wouldn't interrupt us. Instead, she just looked at Mr. Santangelo, waiting to hear what he would say.

"You can just give me a C, and we'll forget about it," I offered.

Mr. Santangelo looked as if he was thinking it over.

"But we want to know about Ethan's fights," one of the boys said.

"Yeah," Jack said. "And I'm hoping Pokie will show us his belly again."

"I'm still waiting for her to tell us about Ticonderoga," Wayne insisted.

"I think you need to go on," Mr. Santangelo sighed.

I sat at my desk, not paying much attention to what the rest of the class was doing with Mr. Santangelo. I knew there were people waiting to hear what I had to say. They wanted to hear *me*. Thérèse LeClerc. How should I begin the next part of the report? I wondered. Maybe . . .

Suddenly, a note that had been making its way around the circle of desks landed in front of me.

"Thérèse, if my mother says it's okay, do you think you could come over for dinner tomorrow night? I'll call you after school. Deborah."

Oh, boy! A fan!

EIGHT

"**W**hy do you always pay all the bills?" I asked my mother the next afternoon on our way to the Churchills'. I eyed the stack of businesslike envelopes, which were going to be dropped off at the post office, on the car seat between us. "Why doesn't Dad do it?"

I held my breath. Would she say it? Would she say, "Well, dear, you see, your father has a little problem. It's nothing for you to worry about, but he can't read so much as the words *a* and *I*."

No, she would not. Instead, she peered out the windshield hunting for the sign that would mean we should turn onto the Churchills' street and laughed. "We'd be living out in the barn if your father took care of paying our bills. He won't even open the envelopes they come in. He just drops them on a shelf somewhere and forgets about them. And I don't want him touching our checkbook. If he were left alone with that thing for even five minutes, it might take me the rest of my life to undo the damage."

"He's . . . he's not good with math?" I asked.

"He's good enough. He just can't be bothered writing

anything down," Mom explained as she pulled into Deborah's driveway.

Can't be bothered or just can't? I thought as my mother exclaimed, "Wow. Look at this house." From the car I couldn't even see the roof, the yellow house was that big, but I could see a huge bay window and some stained glass over the front door and a couple of chimneys. A porch with a fancy wooden trellis hanging from the roof and a railing poking up from the floor ran the length of the front, turned a corner, and continued around the side. There was porch furniture on it—the real stuff, not indoor furniture that was too worn out to use inside anymore.

"Where did you say they're from?" Mom asked as she started to open the car door. "New Jersey? I've never known anyone from there who didn't have money."

Deborah was waiting for us on the porch. "Mom!" she shouted without turning her head. "She's here."

A woman with long, very straight blond (well, almost blond) hair came running down a hallway in back of Deborah. The big gold hoop earrings she was wearing bounced up and down each time she landed on the balls of her bare feet. Her small bony shoulders and chest were covered with a tight black shirt made of that stretchy material you see ballerinas wearing. A gauzy skirt reached down below her knees and swirled around her as she moved.

Suddenly, I noticed that the permanent Aunt Simone had given Mom a few nights back had come out really, really tight. The curls in her hair looked like tiny mattress springs stuck all over her head. And what was that she had on underneath my father's old red plaid jacket? An apron? Of course it was! She practically wore the stinking thing to bed at night. At least it covered up the old housedress my grandmother had given her. Neither Mémé nor Mom feel much need to sew buttons back on things now that there are safety pins that will do the same job with so much less effort.

There weren't any safety pins on Mrs. Churchill, that was for sure.

"Lisa," Mrs. Churchill said, introducing herself to Mom.

"Jeannette," Mom responded.

"I was just on the phone with Brenda Blair. She's arranging for chaperons for the field trip next week," Mrs. Churchill was saying to Mom when Deborah whispered to me, "Let's go up to my room."

She didn't have to ask me twice. Whatever Mom said to Mrs. Churchill was sure to be the wrong thing. I didn't need to be there to hear it.

She took me up some stairs that had a little strip of carpet running down the center of them. The carpeting continued along a hallway that was so big that there was room in it for a table with a statue of a naked fat guy. I liked that the hall was so big, but I think I would have found something else to put on that table.

Deborah's room was off the hall and stuck out over the side porch. It was probably as big as the bedroom my parents shared at home. And it had the kind of things in it you see in bedrooms in the Sears catalog—two beds that matched, curtains and bedspreads that matched, a desk and chair that matched, a bureau and bookcase that matched everything else, a rug (instead of linoleum) that didn't exactly match anything but was right somehow. I realized immediately that in addition to being great looking, Mr. Churchill must be very, very rich. A perfect father.

"Your stuff is great," I told Deborah, figuring that was the polite thing to do.

"I got it while we were still in New Jersey. My mother took me shopping three different times until we found just what I wanted. The last day my father went, too, and we went to lunch in this great . . ."

It was a wonderful story. It could have come right out of a Disney movie, I'm sure. And I wish I'd heard the end of it. But no sooner did she get started when my eye was caught by something. Then I saw it again. And again.

They were everywhere.

Horses. She had them on the curtains and bedspreads. She had horse pillows piled on both beds. She had horse statues lined up along the top of the bookcase. She had a horse-head photo stuck onto the pencil holder on the desk. She had serious-looking pictures of horses in fancy frames on the walls. She had a poster of a running horse hanging on the ceiling over each bed.

"I love this room," Deborah sighed as she threw herself down on one of the horse-covered beds.

I just said, "Yeah."

"Until we can find a farm to keep a horse, this is the only place I can be close to my favorite animal."

I didn't think I had a favorite animal, and if I ever did

I couldn't imagine wanting to be all that close to it. I just said something like "Oh" or "Um."

"Do you remember being little and pretending with your friends that you were all wild horses running through the playground during recess?" Deborah asked.

"Uh . . . no."

There was a long silence after that, which I thought I was to blame for somehow. To get the conversation going again, I nodded toward the extra bed and asked if Deborah had a sister.

"Just a brother. The extra bed is so I can have friends over to spend the night."

"Oh!" Sometime I might get to spend the night in this room!

Underneath the bed Deborah was lying on was a pair of fuzzy slippers with horse heads over the toes. I wondered if her father had bought her those.

"What do you like to do?" Deborah asked.

I shrugged. "Read. Watch television. I used to play a little ice hockey once in a while with my brother and some of our relatives. But then my brother got a concussion when my uncle hit him in the head with a puck, and that kind of scared me off."

"Do you like to draw?"

"I don't know. I've traced a lot of stuff at school. And I've colored things like those potatoes with the leprechaun hats that we did at St. Patrick's Day."

Deborah jumped up off her bed and ran over to her desk. Out of one drawer she pulled a wire-bound tablet of paper without lines. Out of another she took the largest tin of colored pencils I'd ever seen in my life.

"Peggy draws really well," Deborah said as I helped her move the desk up next to one of the beds so we could both sit down to work. "But all she ever wants to do is draw pictures of clothes—especially the things she's going to wear on her first date. She gets really boring sometimes," Deborah complained as she took a book called *Drawing Horses* from her bookcase.

I drew one really skinny horse on pin legs and got pretty bored myself. But Deborah had a little record player (with a picture of a horse cut from a magazine glued to the lid) that I used to play all her records while she drew a couple of horse pictures. One of them had all the horse's body parts labeled in red. It was a gift for me.

We ate supper in a special dining room separate from the kitchen, which I had kind of expected once I'd seen how fancy the house was and that Mrs. Churchill wore earrings when she wasn't going anywhere. We all had little cloth mats under our plates, and the food was brought to the table in special dishes, not the pots. I was looking everything over and reaching for a plate of bread, when Mr. Churchill asked if he could take my hand.

"Of course!" I wanted to shout as he wrapped the warm, firm fingers of his right hand around one of mine. His skin was soft and pink, there was nothing under his fingernails, and he wore a big ring with a dark red stone in it on the finger next to his pinkie. I just happened to notice in passing. I wasn't staring.

"For grace," he explained. "We like to offer a little thanks before we begin to eat."

"Of course," I replied, out loud this time, as if I said grace three times a day and more on Sunday.

There I sat between Mr. Churchill, in his dress shirt, tie, and vest, and Deborah, in a really neat corduroy jumper with some lace around the neck. I held hands with both of them and looked across the table at Mrs. Churchill, looking so strange and beautiful, and Deborah's brother, who I could already tell was smart and serious and not a pain in the neck at all. This, I thought, is the way supper is supposed to be.

Mr. Churchill gave my hand a little squeeze just before he dropped it. While he took a sip of wine out of a real wineglass, Mrs. Churchill asked me if I wanted white milk, chocolate, or strawberry.

"They need to think of one more kind of milk," Deborah said. "Then they'll have one kind for each of the udders."

"Udders?" I repeated.

"You know . . . where the cow's milk comes from," Deborah explained, sounding a little embarrassed.

"Oh! Oh! The tits!"

Everything stopped. Mrs. Churchill just sort of hung above the chair she had been getting out of so she could go out to the kitchen for milk. Deborah sat perfectly still, her eyes popping out of her head, her mouth open. Her older brother held a forkful of the vegetable and brown rice thing we were eating for dinner out in front of his face and stared at it. Only Mr. Churchill was eating his meal as if nothing had happened, and he was doing it very quietly.

"I've . . . I've heard my father say that . . . down in the barn. . . ." I began, my mind working as fast as it could to come up with someone I could blame that slip on.

"Well," Mr. Churchill said slowly, "that is one way of putting it."

Then Mrs. Churchill laughed merrily and asked me once more what kind of milk I wanted, and Deborah asked me if I had to work in the barn. Everything was okay again.

"You haven't met Deborah's brother, Greg, have you, Thérèse?" Mr. Churchill asked, going on with the conversation as if I might be a normal person like him and not somebody who said tit at the dinner table.

I shook my head and looked over at the boy. He gave me a polite smile and nodded. He looked like his father, though without glasses and not as good. The plaid short-sleeved shirt, neatly buttoned and opened at the neck, looked nice, but nothing beats a suit on a guy, if you ask me.

"My brother is in ninth grade at the high school," I said.

"So am I! What's his name?" Greg asked.

"Marcel. Marcel LeClerc."

Greg shook his head.

"You might know him as Marcel LeJerk. That's what they call him on the school bus."

"What's he do for sports?" Greg asked.

"Nothing."

"Is he in band? Student Council?"

"No. He takes shop, though," I offered. "Fifth period. They're making footstools now."

Greg nodded as if he understood something. "I take Latin fifth period. There's no way I'd know your brother."

The bread wasn't white and fluffy like the kind my mother gets but had a hard crust and some things that looked like grain in it. I took a piece to be polite, even though I wasn't very hungry. The eggplant, green peppers, and onions Mrs. Churchill had spooned out onto my plate had kind of taken my appetite away.

"I don't know if Latin is a good choice for a student these days," Mrs. Churchill said to her husband. "The kids are sure to get to Europe at some point. Don't you think it would be better if they took French or German so they can make themselves understood? If I had studied Latin, I don't know how I would have managed that year I spent in Paris when I was in college."

"Latin helps with vocabulary," Mr. Churchill explained. "It will help them with their studies in general. I never regretted the four years I spent studying Latin."

This was too good to be true. Not only could Mr. Churchill read and write, he could do it in Latin.

After they'd talked about Greg's Latin class for a while, they got into a big discussion of some play he was reading in English. Both Mr. and Mrs. Churchill had seen it in New York and wanted to get tickets for the whole family if it was ever in Boston.

"What happened in school with you girls today?" Mrs. Churchill asked us. "What was your poetry discussion about?"

If I'd known someone was going to ask, I might have listened for a minute or two. But I hadn't, and I didn't, so Deborah had to answer the question.

> "I'm nobody. Who are you?
> Are you nobody, too?"

"Emily Dickinson!" Mrs. Churchill exclaimed. "I love her."

"What did Mr. Santangelo have to say about the poem?" Mr. Churchill asked.

"Nothing. He asked us what we thought," Deborah explained.

"I hate it when he does that," I said.

"Oh? Why is that, Thérèse?" Mr. Churchill wanted to know.

That was an awful lot like asking me what I think, which I had just told him I hated. But I liked the way he looked at a person when he talked to her, and to keep him doing that I was going to have to talk back.

So, I said, "Well, a bunch of kids said we liked the poem because it was short. Then Mr. Santangelo got upset with us because we're not supposed to like poems because they're short. We're supposed to like them for some other reason. But he wouldn't tell us what that other reason is. Then he got upset because we didn't know it."

Mr. Churchill nodded thoughtfully.

So far, so good. I decided to add a little more. "Should he ask us what we think, and then get mad at us for thinking it?"

"You're a hundred percent right, Thérèse," Mr. Churchill agreed. "He should be telling you what he wants you to think."

I was right—a hundred percent! I wondered if there was any chance that we could say grace again after supper and hold hands some more.

But supper was over way too fast. Before I knew it, Mr. Churchill went off to the special little room they had for watching television so he could watch the *CBS Evening News* and read the newspaper. Deborah and I were alone in the living room where she sat down at the piano and played the theme music to every horsie television show ever made. She played those pieces over and over, and even though she sounded good, there's only so long I can listen to the same things.

I wandered around looking at the books on the shelves built into the walls and the magazines on all the little tables until I was close enough to the hallway leading to the TV room to hear Walter Cronkite announcing how many people had died in Vietnam the past week. He called them casualty figures. I was always wondering if *casualty* meant dead *and* wounded or just dead. Because if it meant dead *and* wounded then our side having twenty-seven casualties, as Walter Cronkite said that night, wasn't bad at all. Maybe only ten or twelve of those guys were actually dead, and the others would all get better. Of course, if *casualty* meant dead, it was still good because we had only twenty-seven casualties compared to the Viet Cong, who had over a hundred. We must be winning.

I was just thinking that asking Mr. Churchill what *casualty* meant would be a good excuse to go into that little room and talk to him, when Deborah's mother announced that it was time for me to go home. I got to sit next to him in the Churchills' fancy station wagon without having to do anything at all. On top of everything else, when we saw Brownie trotting along the side of the road, far from home, not only did Mr. Churchill not swerve all over the place trying to hit him, he didn't swear, he didn't pound the steering wheel with the flat of his hand, he didn't so much as blink.

I thought, What a man, eh?

NINE

There are so many great stories about how awful Ethan Allen was that it's hard to write them all down. At lunch Friday, I had my report with me and one of those Ticonderoga pencils so I could keep working when I wasn't hunting for onions in my lasagna or picking the canned fruit out of my Jell-O.

At the same time, though, I was wondering if maybe Deborah would come sit with me so everyone could see us together. Or would she come up to me during recess after lunch, which would really be better, anyway, because I was kind of busy. Before school she had asked me if I thought we'd see any horses at Fort Ticonderoga, and I'd said, "Sure hope so!" which I hoped would keep her friendly long enough to invite me over one more time for dinner with her dad. In addition to all that, I was trying to keep an eye on Mr. Santangelo. He sometimes went up to kids at lunchtime and offered to help them with their math, which was nice, I suppose, but I would just as soon he didn't.

So I never saw Tammy and Lynn coming. They were just all of a sudden sitting on either side of me.

"What did you think of Deborah's room? Isn't it great?" Tammy asked.

"Y-e-e-es," I said slowly, wondering what was up.

"Did you see all the record albums her parents have? It's all awful stuff, but there sure are a lot of them," Tammy said.

"They have a dishwasher."

"And two phones."

"Her mother is sooo cool. You should see her dance. She can do everything."

They seemed to be talking to each other until Lynn brought up Greg. "Her brother's cute, isn't he?" she said to me.

"I suppose."

"Did he say anything about anybody?" Tammy asked.

"His Latin teacher."

Tammy shook her head. "Did he talk about anybody we know? Any of us?"

"Oh, no. Why would he?"

Tammy and Lynn looked at each other and laughed.

"Peggy thinks Greg is the secret admirer who wrote to *The Polka Hour* about her birthday," Tammy told me.

"I told her she was nuts if she thought a high school kid was going to have a crush on her, especially Greg *Churchill*," Lynn said. "But she doesn't think there's anybody who's too good for her."

"Maybe Prince Charles called *The Polka Hour* about her from England," Tammy suggested.

"I . . . uh . . . would be kind of surprised if it was a prince or Greg Churchill," was all I could think of to say while Tammy and Lynn laughed.

"Have you heard anything?" Tammy asked. "Who do you think it could be?"

I looked around the cafeteria until I found Peggy sitting next to Yvette and Deborah. Peggy was poking at the food on her tray and looking bored while Yvette and Deborah leaned toward each other, deep in some sort of conversation. Then my eyes wandered around from boy to boy. Jack would be a good secret admirer for Peggy. I wished he'd thought of writing into the radio station about her instead of me. A scrawny third or fourth grader would be good, too. Or what about the kid in fifth grade who . . .

I was distracted by Pokie, who was waving at me, trying to get my attention. Once he knew he had my eye he pointed to the red ball he was clutching under one arm, then at me and back at himself. He was letting me know that he had plans for us to play kickball during recess.

"I heard it's Pokie," I said suddenly.

"Pokie! He's always liked *you!*" Tammy reminded me.

I tried to look sad. "He's been acting odd lately. . . ."

"Lately?" Lynn broke in. "It would be odd for him not to act odd. He's such a goofball."

I should have belted her for that, but I knew all that would do was make me look foolish since it was so obvious she was right.

"Well," I said, as if Lynn were my best friend instead of someone who up to that moment had only spoken to me if she absolutely had to, "a guy would have to be a goofball to be Peggy's secret admirer, wouldn't he?"

"That's for sure," she agreed as Tammy turned around, leaned toward another table, and started whispering to some girls who were sitting there.

I felt as if I'd accomplished something even though my report was untouched. A good job done, I thought as Tammy and Lynn jumped up and ran over to join Peggy for recess.

" 'In addition to swearing a lot, Ethan Allen drank a lot,' " was the first thing I read at the very beginning of the next part of my oral report.

"Really?" Jack asked.

I knew that would get his attention, anyway, and it got a lot of other people's, too.

"Really," I said before going back to my report.

"Hanging around in taverns, drinking, shooting off his mouth about religion and the local authorities got him in trouble when he was back in Connecticut. In fact, when he was living in Massachusetts, a minister once asked him to stop being such a bad influence on his neighbors. But up in the New Hampshire Grants people actually liked bad influences. After his trip to Albany to see that court case I told you about last time, he went to the local tavern near where he was living in the Grants. He told everyone what happened, maybe mentioned that the gods of the hills weren't the gods of the valleys a few times, and said they needed to put up a fight. The next thing you know, everybody was agreeing to form a militia to protect their farms from the New Yorkers. And then they voted to make Ethan its leader. They made him a colonel just like Colonel Hogan on *Hogan's Heroes*."

"Hey, that's a good show," Pokie broke in.

"Yeah, yeah. Anyway, a militia is like a little army that's only used when there's an emergency, which is what Ethan and his new neighbors thought they had on their hands. Only governments, like a state or a country, are supposed to start armies. The farmers didn't have the legal right to start a militia, and Ethan didn't have the legal right to lead it. That made them all outlaws."

"Like Robin Hood," Wayne said.

"Except they didn't dress so weird," I said without looking up from my papers.

"Those outlaws were the Green Mountain Boys. They didn't have uniforms, they just stuck a piece of a fir branch in their hats so they would all recognize each other if they met in the woods or something. They didn't line up and go marching around or practice being soldiers.

"Instead, this is how they worked. Sometimes New Yorkers would send surveyors into the Grants to map out land they were planning to take over. Sometimes they'd try to convince a farmer that he could only keep his farm if he bought it a second time—from a New Yorker. Sometimes a New York posse would come into the mountains to put a farmer off his land. Whenever a Grantsman was threatened, word would go out, and the Green Mountain Boys would stop whatever they were doing on their own farms and take off. They'd capture the New Yorkers and hold a little trial.

"Ethan loved the trials. He would act as the prosecuting attorney *and* the judge so he could both give a fancy speech listing all the things the New Yorkers had done wrong and decide the punishment. There was always punishment because Ethan always found them guilty of whatever he charged them with. Then the defendant might be tied to a tree and beaten for a while before he was sent home full of tales of how dangerous the Green Mountains were.

"Once Ethan and the Boys captured two sheriffs from New York. Ethan locked them up in separate rooms on different sides of a building. During the night he hung something that looked like a person from a tree outside of each of their windows. The next morning he told each one of them that the other one had been hung. Then they were both allowed to escape at different times so that they wouldn't meet each other and would go home still believing (and telling everyone they knew) that Ethan and the Green Mountain Boys were murderers.

"But Ethan never killed a New Yorker. He strapped one to the top of a pole outside a tavern and left him there for a few hours so everyone could come by and laugh at him. He burned the roofs off the houses of people who sympathized with the New Yorkers. He wrote letters to the newspapers in Connecticut and pamphlets insisting that the poor farmers in the Grants had a right to their land. He spoke for those farmers. But he didn't kill anybody.

"And, of course, he swore a lot.

"Once he swore at a New Yorker his men had captured in the Grants.

" 'Colonel Allen, you do blaspheme so,' the man said to him.

" 'Blaspheme? Blaspheme?' Ethan repeated. 'I'll give you blasphemy!'

"Which was when he really started ripping.

"The New York government finally offered a reward for Ethan and a few of the better-known Green Mountain Boys, some of them being his relatives. You'd think that would make him sorry for the things he'd done. Or at least worried. But Ethan didn't know the meaning of the word *sorry* or *worry*, either. He turned around and had some posters made up saying he was offering a reward for the capture of some of the New Yorkers who'd been taking Grantsmen to court.

"He laughed at his enemies, and he made other people laugh at them, too. He made the powerful New

Yorkers look foolish, and when they looked foolish they didn't seem so powerful.

"Some people say that one day Ethan got on his horse and rode to Albany, the capital of New York. He walked into a tavern, sat down under a poster advertising the reward for his capture, and had himself a drink. Then he got up and went home. Just to show he could.

"Ethan was becoming so famous for the writing he was doing pleading the Grantsmen's case—and for swearing and terrifying people—that just knowing he was somewhere nearby was enough to send a New Yorker who had wandered into the Green Mountains running for home. Things went on like that for five years. It would have gone on longer, but war broke out between the colonies and Great Britain, and now the people in the Grants had another problem.

"After five years of fighting against the colony that was supposed to rule them, they didn't feel much connection to it or any of the other colonies that were rebelling. They were sort of on their own. Were they going to join the fight against the king? Or were they going to fight with him?"

I paused, held my breath, and finally looked up to see how everyone was doing. They were all watching me. But it wasn't that dumb, "is-it-over-yet?" look I usually got from them when I was reading what I'd written. People were leaning forward across their desks toward me, as if being that much closer would make them hear better. And what's more, I realized that I had read a big chunk of report with no one trying to interrupt me.

If you can make an oral report interesting enough—say, about drinking, swearing, and generally getting in trouble—people will listen. Personally, I like it when people listen.

I turned to Mr. Santangelo. "I'm sorry, Mr. Santangelo. I wasn't able to finish. There's just so much to say. I'll give another report if I can have some more time to prepare."

"Can you have more time to prepare your report? Of course you can! This is a school, isn't it?" Mr. Santangelo exclaimed.

There were no complaints that time about my getting another chance. I could almost feel a prickly sensation along my skin as I sat down, though whether it was because I had done so well or was going to get to do it again I can't say.

"You know, Mr. Santangelo, it's almost as if Ethan and the Green Mountain Boys were guerrilla warriors making quick, short attacks on their enemies instead of fighting regular battles, isn't it?" Wayne suggested.

"Good comparison, Wayne. Excellent point," Mr. Santangelo told him, right in front of all of us.

The prickly sensation was gone. Instead, I felt as if I was trying to get over sitting on a tack. I had made any number of excellent points just moments before, but had Mr. Santangelo noticed? No, he had not. I could have kicked myself for not thinking of that guerrilla thing. It would have made me look brilliant.

Then I saw Pokie's face, the squinting eyes, the pursed lips, the look of confusion.

Peggy saw it, too. "Not the giant monkey, you idiot," she said to him. "The people who don't fight in regular military groups. They raid their enemies instead of fighting formal battles. They often don't belong to regular armies. They . . ."

Peggy went on and on. It was as if there was nothing she didn't know about guerrillas. She must have read our entire *Weekly Reader*, not just under the pictures.

"Next report is on the Battle at Fort Ti!" I announced when it looked as if she would never shut up.

The person giving the oral report should always have the last word.

• • •

Wayne had a brilliant idea. He really did. We were going on our field trip to Fort Ticonderoga the next Tuesday. Why doesn't Tessy give her report at the fort? he asked. That's why everyone thinks he's so smart. It's because he is. I'd be talking right there, at the fort. It would be so dramatic and exciting. And there'd be chaperons there. And they'd have to listen to me.

Was I ever sorry I had told Mr. Santangelo I should get a B if I finished the report. I should have tried for a B+ at the very least.

The field trip was making Mr. Santangelo even more popular than he had been before. Everyone forgot about the poems he made us write to send to Mrs. Ford and her daughter and just thought about the fact that we were going on the longest bus ride of our lives and we owed it all to him.

I can't say I was particularly looking forward to the bus ride since I was probably going to have to sit with Pokie. Not that I was disappointed. It wasn't as if I was Deborah and used to having smart, popular kids like Wayne hanging around me. It wasn't as if I expected someone like Mr. Santangelo or Mrs. Churchill to pick someone like me to sit next to. I knew better.

Which was the strange thing about the Ethan Allen report. I got to do what everyone thought was the best report. That kind of thing just doesn't happen to me. But I hadn't wanted it. And having to do something I don't want to do is exactly the kind of thing that happens to me all the time. So in a weird sort of way, I should have expected it.

TEN

The best part of going to church on Sundays is stopping for jelly doughnuts at the bakery on the way home. Wondering what kind of tool they use to get that thick, sweet raspberry jelly inside those perfect little balls with their incredibly thin, crisply fried crust covered with sugar (granulated, not powdered) has often been the only thing that kept me awake through many a mind-numbing sermon.

The bakery is what gets my father into town on Sundays, too. He's told us several times that he doesn't care what Mom says, if the bakery ever closes he's through spending an hour every week sitting in church on a hard bench listening to a priest who has no more common sense than he does. However, he can't be trusted to buy jelly doughnuts. He's been known to come out of the bakery with crullers or those awful custard-filled cakes, so on the Sunday before our field trip Marcel went in with him to keep an eye on him. That's why he was able to run back to the car to explain why Dad was still hanging around in front of the bakery, holding our white bakery bag, and yakking with Mr. Falcowski.

"Brownie ate two of Mr. Falcowski's sheep!" Marcel announced. "Can you believe it? Two."

"I can't believe he ate one," Mom said as we watched Dad shake his head soberly while Mr. Falcowski's mouth opened and shut, opened and shut, and he pounded the air with his fist.

"Mr. Falcowski doesn't look as if he's been to church, if you ask me," I observed as he took off his torn cap and hit the knee of his dirty coveralls with it. "He didn't have to waste his whole Sunday morning pretending to listen to a sermon in order to get a lousy doughnut."

"When we're old coots like Falcowski, we'll be able to do whatever we want, too," Marcel promised.

"*Mr.* Falcowski to you," Mom told him as Dad finally headed toward our car.

Dad pulled open the car door with a jerk and threw the bakery bag on the seat, which is very hard on jelly doughnuts. He was breathing heavily as he slid behind the wheel and started the car.

"Well?" Mom said.

The only repeatable word in Dad's response was "dog."

"He didn't actually eat the sheep, did he?" Mom asked, not sounding very convinced.

"Of course he didn't! No dog's hungry enough to eat two sheep! He killed them for the fun of it! LaFontaine, he's going to have to do something about that goddamn dog now!"

"Roland," Mom said quietly. "We just came from church."

135

Dad crossed himself, which he does every now and then. He calls it a bad habit. "Falcowski should call the state police, him. A dog that kills farm animals is like a criminal."

"What's he going to do?" Marcel asked. "Will the cops come out and shoot the dog?"

"Oh, he's going to go *talk* to LaFontaine. Everybody for miles around has *talked* to LaFontaine!"

"Why is Mr. Falcowski so sure it was Brownie?" I asked. "There are lots of dogs around here. And maybe it was a wild animal. Did anybody think of that?"

"She's right, Dad. It could have been a chipmunk," Marcel suggested. "There are lots of them around here, too."

"It could have been a herd of chipmunks! But it wasn't! It was Brownie!"

"Wow. Sheep. Two of them," Marcel said. He shook his head, obviously impressed.

"Ah, sheep are dumb animals. They probably just stood there and let the dog rip them apart. If Brownie takes down one of my cows, I'll tip my hat to him. I'll kill him, me, but I'll tip my hat first."

"You know, *if* Brownie did this, he's in the wrong because he's doing the killing. But if you kill Brownie, then *you'll* be in the wrong because you'll be doing the killing," I said to Dad.

I could see Dad looking at me in the rearview mirror. "You! You always take the dog's side!" he complained.

"It just seems as if there's some kind of rule you'd be breaking if you killed Brownie," I explained, though that wasn't explaining much since I didn't know what the rule was. "You know how there are laws the government makes and we can go to jail for breaking them? Well, maybe there are other laws the government doesn't make and doesn't enforce, but we're still supposed to follow them. I just wish you wouldn't kill that dog, Dad."

Dad didn't say anything after that, but when he stopped at an intersection he reached back and patted my leg. It wasn't a promise, but I thought it was a good sign.

The phone was ringing when we got home. Phone calls on Sunday mornings are never a good thing. Who calls just to chat on a Sunday morning? People are either tied up with church, or they assume everyone else is. At the very least, a phone call before noon on Sunday means an unexpected visit from one of your least-favorite relatives.

Mom still had the receiver trapped between her shoulder and ear when I got into the kitchen after changing my clothes. She already had put on an apron over her good dress. She had turned the burner on under the pot of potatoes and water she had fixed before church and was checking the pork roast that had been cooking in the oven for a couple of hours.

"No, Brenda, I really don't think I can. Roland needs me to help with the planting. . . . Oh, there are lots of people who love doing that sort of thing. . . . No? . . . I really think you should try someone else. . . . Just two-fifty for the admission? . . . That is tempting. . . . No, I don't think so. . . . Thanks for thinking of me."

She banged the receiver into the cradle. "That woman sets my teeth on edge."

"Who was it?" Dad asked. He had switched to an undershirt and a pair of work pants and was wandering around the kitchen in his sock feet, looking for something to eat while dinner was cooking.

"Brenda Blair."

Dad laughed. "A good woman, eh?"

"The best," Mom told him.

"What did she want?" Dad asked as he rooted around in the bakery bag.

"She wants me to go on this field trip to Ticonderoga on Tuesday. One of the chaperons canceled and now she has only that lawyer's wife—Lisa Churchill—and herself. I don't want to go anywhere with them. Get on a bus with twenty-seven screaming kids and Brenda Blair? When hell freezes over." Mom laughed.

"Mr. Churchill's a lawyer? No wonder he always looks so good," I said.

Mom pointed at Dad. "Take a look at your father, Tess. Now, *that's* a good-looking man."

Dad turned his head so he could show off his profile. It couldn't begin to compete with Mr. Churchill's.

"She was doing her best to make me feel guilty, too— telling me that they'll have to cancel the field trip if they don't find another parent to go," Mom explained to Dad.

"Mom!" I wailed. "You're not going to make them cancel, are you?"

"They're not going to cancel," she assured me as she

snapped the metal binding holding the lid onto a jar of her pickles. "Someone will go. Someone always goes to those things."

"How do you know? We've never had a decent field trip before. Maybe people won't go to them all the time," I objected.

"Ah, Brenda can get her husband to go, if she has to. He does whatever she tells him to. Set the table, Tess," Mom ordered.

The metal drawer in the white porcelain cabinet we used for storing dishes and silverware squealed as I opened it. "He won't come. No father has ever come to anything at school. You wait and see, we're not going to be able to go."

I threw the forks and spoons across the table, then pulled the plates off their metal shelf.

You can bet that if she were my real mother she'd go, I thought as I slid things into their proper places at the table and fought the giant, humongous knot of tears caught in my chest. If I could grow up with my real parents, like Deborah was, instead of whoever to hell these people were, I wouldn't have to beg to keep my mother from ruining a simple field trip. Why couldn't she have ruined one of those walks through the cemetery we were always being dragged on? No! That might have made me happy!

"Our bébé is sad," Dad cooed as he offered me the last of the doughnut he'd been eating—the part without any jelly. I knocked his hand out of my way with my arm.

"Not everything can go her way, Roland."

"Nothing goes my way!"

Dad looked at Mom. "Why can't you go, Jeannette?"

"Because I don't want to. I hate being with those snobby mothers who run everything at the school. I'd have to spend the whole day with Brenda."

"Does this mean I can stop going to school because I don't want to spend the whole day—every day—with Peggy?" I asked.

Mom sighed one of her "I'm trying to keep from killing you" sighs. "No, it does not."

"So you don't have to do what you don't want to do, but I do. Nobody should be able to make an unequal rule like that just because they have money and power."

Dad laughed so hard Mom had to hit him on the back to keep him from choking on that doughnut end I hadn't wanted. Finally, he wiped his eyes and said to me, "Money?"

Mom was grinning, too. "Power? Does someone around here have 'power'?"

Dad laid his arm across my shoulders and gave them a squeeze. "I'm so happy, me, that someone thinks I am a rich and powerful man."

He kept his arm around me, and he turned us both so we were facing Mom. "How can you say no to our little girl?"

Mom probably does have trouble saying no to little girls. I, however, was about the same size as Mrs. Blair, and she had no problem saying no to either one of us.

"Why don't *you* go?" she asked Dad.

Dad dropped his arm and stepped back, shocked. "Men don't go to things at school!"

"Mom!"

"Oh, look at her," Dad said as he kissed a tear off my cheek.

"Okay, okay," Mom finally agreed, though it was clear from her tone that she was being made to suffer horribly, and I was to blame.

I thought about hugging her, something kind of quick and not too close. Isn't that what you're supposed to do when your mother finally agrees to do something she should have done anyway? But she was squatting down looking for the pan she uses for gravy, then she had to find her wooden spoon, and then she was hacking at the pork roast with the carving knife. By the time it was safe to get near her, I didn't feel like it anymore.

I went off to my room to work on my report for a while before we ate.

"The Green Mountain Boys," I wrote, "had been fighting the New Yorkers for five years when the Revolution broke out like a rash. . . ."

I stopped, crossed out "like a rash," and wrote "like smallpox." I liked that much better.

"Now the New Hampshire Grants weren't just trapped between New Hampshire and New York, they were also trapped between the American colonies to the south and Canada to the north. That wouldn't have been so bad if Canada was still owned by France. But it wasn't. The British had chased the French government out of Canada, which is what the French and Indian War was all about. Now they had all kinds of military forces up there ready and able to invade the colonies. The New Hampshire Grants were all that was in their way. Because the New Hampshire Grants really weren't controlled by any government, they didn't have any kind of official organization to help if they were attacked. All they had were the Green Mountain Boys.

"Lake Champlain ran between the Grants and New York right toward Massachusetts and Connecticut, like a main road. It was protected by two British forts at Ticonderoga and Crown Point, both on the New York side. If the British invaded from Canada, the lake would be their easiest route and they could take control of the Grants on their way. It would be a good idea for the Green Mountain Boys to side with them to protect their property and families.

"But the Green Mountain Boys had come to the Grants from colonies like Connecticut, Massachusetts, and Rhode Island. If they sided with the British, they'd be fighting against their relatives and neighbors in the colonies.

"What did Ethan think about all this? 'Ever since I arrived to a state of manhood,' he said, 'and acquainted myself with the general history of mankind, I have felt a sincere passion for liberty. The history of nations doomed to perpetual slavery, in consequence of yielding up to tyrants their natural born liberties, I read with a sort of philosophical horror . . .' The young man who had read those books about rebelling against governments that didn't protect your rights under those unwritten natural laws now decided, many years later, that he would have to do just that."

Not bad, I thought. Especially that part about having natural born liberties. I wouldn't mind having a few of those myself.

I had another day and a half to finish my writing. That ought to give me time to get things just the way I wanted them. I knew how I wanted everything to be at the fort. Giving the report there was going to be almost like being in a movie, except, of course, we wouldn't have any costumes or props or makeup people or hairdressers.

I'd forgotten about my mother's hair. Well, it couldn't be helped. Maybe if she washed it two or three times a day, some of Aunt Simone's perm would have gone down the drain by Tuesday.

ELEVEN

Mr. Santangelo didn't even try to get any-one to sit down the Tuesday morning of the field trip. He didn't even try to get us to say the Pledge of Allegiance or do any of the other things we do every morning.

Not that I think he should have, but the point I'm try-ing to make is that we were all in the room, some stand-ing up inside our circle of chairs, some sitting on our desktops. Peggy, I think, was sitting on a chair, but it wasn't hers. She was part of the group of girls around Deborah. Everyone was talking and looking at one another's lunches. The girls were trying to decide whether they wanted to wear their sweaters or knot them around their waists. Jack was laughing and pointing across the room toward Pokie, who had stuck a little pine branch behind his ear (he didn't have a hat) so he could pretend to be a Green Mountain Boy. I felt sorry for Pokie, but I also wanted to shake him and say, "Don't you think before you do some-thing stupid like that?"

Our classroom door was open, and I caught the sound

of something going on out in the hallway. So did a few of the other kids. Heads began to turn.

"Is everyone here?" Mr. Santangelo asked. "Maybe I should take attendance."

I looked over toward the door where I could see a blue-and-green plaid skirt that I knew had to be Mrs. Blair's. She must have a closet full of plaid skirts, each one with a co-ordinating pullover sweater.

"Yes. I should definitely take attendance."

I saw Mrs. Churchill's back. She was wearing blue jeans and one of those print shirts from India. I hoped my mother wasn't wearing the dress she wore to church on Sunday. It would be too nice. But if she didn't wear that, what would she wear? She didn't have a print shirt from India, and she wouldn't wear a plaid skirt, even if she had one, because Mrs. Blair wore them.

Mr. Santangelo started calling out names that no one answered to because Mrs. Blair had stuck her big halo of teased hair into the classroom. She trotted in after it, her penny loafers tapping across the gray-and-white tile floor. Mrs. Churchill still had her back to us and was talking to someone just out of sight in the hall. She turned around, a big smile on her face, the biggest and fanciest camera I'd ever seen in real life dangling from one shoulder, and followed Mrs. Blair into the room. And behind her came . . . my father.

That would have been awful enough all by itself, but to add to the shock, he was wearing the pants to the old suit he wears to funerals and weddings and his one white dress shirt. The top button was undone so the whole world could see the top of his undershirt, and his pack of Marlboros was visible through his breast pocket. Over that he had a shapeless gray jacket I hadn't seen since Marcel had worn it at Halloween.

"Hey! Rolie's here!" Jack shouted. "Rolie's going with us!"

If it had ever occurred to me to have a worst nightmare, having Dad show up with the field trip chaperons would have been it. I had to clutch my desk to keep from sliding under it.

Mr. Santangelo gave up immediately and let Mrs. Blair take over getting us organized with our lunches and admission money. I was still staring, openmouthed, at Dad when she got us lined up against the wall to head out to the bus.

"Tante Joséphine," Dad whispered to me as we marched down the hall toward the school's main entrance. "She had some kind of spell last night, her. Your mother is taking her to the doctor."

He was so close to me that I could see the little bit of white shaving cream that he'd missed washing off under his jaw. The sweet, sharp scent of the stuff still clung to him.

"It's just gas!" I complained. "She's going to give one raunchy, disgusting burp and be all better!"

People started laughing from in front and behind me, and both Mrs. Blair and Mrs. Churchill turned around to look.

"Thérèse, keep your voice down," Dad managed to say, just loudly enough to make sure everyone heard him.

I grabbed the first seat I saw on the bus and pressed myself against the window. My father stood in the aisle, blocking everyone while he stared toward the back of the bus.

"Jacques!" he bellowed. *"Qu'est-ce que tu fait?"*

"Nothing!" Jack yelled back. "I'm not doing anything."

"Venez-ici!" Dad ordered. "Don't make me go back there and get you."

"But I want to sit in the back."

Dad took off down the aisle.

Maybe he won't come back, I thought hopefully. He's definitely a back-of-the-bus kind of guy. He could just stay back there and talk dirty with the boys the whole trip and think he'd had a great time.

But the back of the bus erupted into a chorus of "Frère Jacques" repeated over and over. Mr. Santangelo and the bus driver both ended up back there while Mrs. Blair stood at the front with her arms crossed, looking like an armed guard.

"I only hit him because he said I was fat," Jack complained as Dad and Mr. Santangelo pushed and pulled him up toward our seat. Dad made himself comfortable next to me and pulled Jack down onto the seat with him.

"You hit everybody who says you're fat?" Dad asked.

"Yeah."

"You must not do a very good job or they'd stop. You better think of something else to do, eh? Something you can do better?"

"I hit everybody who calls me Jacques, too," Jack said. He looked, sitting on the other side of my father, a lot like I felt.

"You better be able to hit better than you did just now, you, if you're going to take a swing at me," Dad warned.

"Il est un bon jour, n'est-ce pas?" Mrs. Churchill called out to my father from two seats ahead of us as the bus started to move. Then she turned to me. "Thérèse, you never told us your father spoke French. I'm so excited. It's been years since I've had anyone to speak French with. I can't wait until we get there."

I sat up. Did that mean Mrs. Churchill and Deborah were going to stay with us during the field trip? I looked at my father. Did it?

"I've got a cow down in my barn, me, that can talk French out her backside better than that woman can," Dad whispered to me out of the corner of his mouth after Mrs. Churchill turned around.

"What are you talking about? She lived in Paris for a whole year," I told him.

"Ah. That explains the awful accent."

There was all kinds of yelling going on. A lot of it came from Peggy. Pokie was sitting behind her, and she kept screeching at him to stay away from her, which made me suspect that my suggestion that he was her *Polka Hour* admirer had gotten back to her. In addition, the bus itself hummed and rattled so I could hardly hear Jack screaming to his friends in the backseats. But, still, Mr. Santangelo suggested I give some of my oral report before we arrived at the fort.

"I can't."

"What's that?" Mr. Santangelo shouted.

"I can't read while I'm moving."

"Troop movements? You want to tell us about troop movements?"

"No, I . . ."

"She pukes if she reads while she's moving!" Dad yelled as the bus pulled up to an intersection and stopped for a moment, its engine idling quietly.

"Oh," Mr. Santangelo replied. He looked over to where I had turned to press one of my hot cheeks against the cold glass of the bus window. "So do I."

It was a good thing I hadn't been looking forward to the bus ride.

We had to sit in the bus next to the lake and wait for the ferry to come back from New York to take us over to Ticonderoga. The bus wasn't running at that point so we could hear Mrs. Blair and Peggy squeal and carry on about whether or not they could see the fort from their seats. Whatever it was they were looking at, it wasn't Fort Ti. It's a giant, stone, castlelike thing all by itself on a piece of land that sticks out into Lake Champlain, but you just can't see it from where you get on the ferry on the Vermont side of the lake. On other parts of the New York coast you can see buildings looking like little dots someone put in with a set of colored pencils like Deborah's. But, no matter what Peggy says, the biggest thing there is hidden by trees and the way the coast curves on that side of the lake.

"What a great place for an ambush," I said out loud.

Mrs. Blair patted her great big chest with one hand so that everyone got a chance to see that her bracelet and necklace matched. "What a tho-o-ought!" she replied, sounding just like Peggy.

"Ambush!" Jack roared, cutting it off abruptly when Dad gave him an elbow in the chest.

I spoke directly to Mrs. Blair so she had to pay attention and listen to every word I said. "You're a British soldier coming down the lake from Canada, sailing along, not seeing a thing, maybe daydreaming because so little's going on. When you get around that point over there . . . Kaboom! There were over a hundred cannons in that fort when the Green Mountain Boys captured it, you know."

"It's such a nice day. Let's think about something else," Mrs. Blair suggested.

"Yeah, let's not think about body parts floating on top of the lake," Jack said, which, of course, meant that half the people on the bus had to shout out that they could see feet and heads and rear ends bobbing on the water.

The driver turned the engine off again once we were on the ferry, and Mrs. Blair stood up and guarded the door so we had to stay on the bus even while we were waiting for the other vehicles to park. Mr. Santangelo turned in his seat and read aloud from a brochure. His voice kept getting louder and louder, but the roar in the bus always increased just enough to drown him out.

"Shut up!"

A silence hit us so suddenly it was as if a giant concrete block had dropped on the bus, snuffing out anything that could make a sound.

"I want to hear what the man has to say," Dad said.

I looked over at his watch. It wasn't even nine-thirty.

"Thank you," Mr. Santangelo said nervously. Then he looked down at his brochure. "Here's something about how the fort was built . . . nah, we don't need to know that. Oh! Here's something about where they stored their gunpowder . . . we can skip that . . . Look at this—three whole paragraphs on the different classifications of rocks under the fort! Maybe . . ."

"Don't you have anything you can read to us about Ethan Allen?" Wayne asked. "He's why we're here."

"We're here to goof off for a day," Jack reminded him.

"No, you are not," Mr. Santangelo objected. "The geology and geography of this area are perfectly legitimate fields of study, and I want . . ."

"Have Tessy give some of her report now," Pokie suggested. "*Please.*"

"Tessy . . . Tessy . . . Tessy . . ."

It sounded as if they were singing—a good song, too. I could have listened to it all the way across the lake and up the road to the fort. Dad joined in and clapped his hands to "Thérèse . . . Thérèse . . . Thérèse . . ." I sat there with my head down, this big smile on my face, the way I'd seen other girls do so many times when people were making a fuss over them.

But when people carry on about you like that you have to do something or they start getting mean. Once I started hearing questions like "What's wrong with her?" and "Somebody make her do something" floating up from the back of the bus, I got nervous and pulled out my papers, figuring I'd just read the first few paragraphs and end with the line about Ethan deciding to rebel against the British government.

"Well, everybody knew that," Peggy said when I stopped.

There was some grumbling as Mrs. Blair smiled proudly at her little girl.

"Yeah!" Jack barked. "Tell us some more of that bad stuff about Ethan, Tess. That's what you're good at. If we wanted to hear boring stuff about how Lake Champlain is like a main road, we might as well have let Mr. SanTan read us his brochure."

I leaned across Dad so I could make sure Jack heard what I had to say to him. "If you weren't so stupid, you'd understand that a good oral report has to include *all* the facts."

"She called me stupid!" Jack howled just before he dived for me.

Dad leaned forward enough to keep us apart.

"She was just getting started," Dad told him. "You can

tell she hasn't gotten to the main part of the story, right?"
Then he turned to me. "Go on."

I didn't want to go on. I wanted to wait for the fort.
That was my plan.

"Show them," he said when I didn't speak up right
away. "Go on."

"Not now," I tried to say without moving my lips.

"It's all right, bébé. You're good," he said.

"Yeah, bébé, you're go-o-od," Jack repeated just before
my father gave him a shove.

Won't this ferry ever start moving? I thought as I
looked through what I'd written trying to find some little
thing I could read them that would still leave the best stuff
for inside the fort. I'd seen a sign saying the ride across the
lake was only supposed to last three minutes. It didn't say
how long you had to wait to get going.

"All right," I sighed.

"The people who lived near the fort were always going
in and out, doing business with the soldiers there. A
few weeks after the Battles of Lexington and Concord—which we lost, by the way, even though none of
our social studies books make a big point of mentioning it—a Green Mountain Boy was sent into Fort
Ticonderoga. He told the British soldiers he wanted to
see the barber there for a shave. He came out with the
news that the soldiers in the fort hadn't received word
yet that the colonies and the British were fighting.

They weren't expecting anyone to attack them because they didn't know a war was going on. That night three hundred Green Mountain Boys arrived. So did someone else."

I stopped and looked up. "To find out who it was, listen to the rest of the report in the fort."

There were a bunch of groans, and Dad said, "No, no, no. That's not the way you tell a story. You should know better than that, you."

As the ferry's engine started and we moved out onto the lake, Dad leaned toward the aisle as if he was the one who knew what he was talking about. " 'That night, three hundred'—what were they? Green Mountain Boys?—'arrived,' " he repeated. " 'So did someone else.' "

Then he turned and pointed at me, indicating to everyone around us that I was supposed to go on.

"Ethan Allen wasn't the only person who thought the colonists should capture Fort Ticonderoga. There were little groups here and there organizing the colonists in the fight against the British. Ethan and the Green Mountain Boys were given the authority to attack by a group in Connecticut, but a group in Massachusetts had given it to another man.

"He was a militia captain in New Haven, Connecticut. That means he was a captain in a real militia that had been formed by the government that ran the colony of Connecticut, unlike the Green Mountain Boys, who just decided one night in a bar that they would call themselves a militia. The militia captain had been promoted to colonel special so he could lead the attack on Fort Ticonderoga. That means he was a real colonel, unlike Ethan Allen, who was just a colonel because the Green Mountain Boys said so. The militia captain had experience fighting the British, who were being attacked in Boston by the Americans, unlike Ethan Allen, who had just been chasing surveyors, sheriffs, and those sorts through the woods.

"He was even a couple of years younger than Ethan, who was thirty-seven by then. This guy was better than Ethan in every way, and if I'd been a Green Mountain Boy I would have thanked my lucky stars that Benedict Arnold showed up just hours before I was supposed to attack a real fort and offered to run the whole show."

"Benedict Arnold!" several people shouted as the ferry was bumping against whatever ferries bump against when they reach shore.

"The traitor?"

The bus started to roll off the ferry, so I quickly folded my papers and stuck them back in my pocket. I figured that since the whole world knew I puked when I read in a moving vehicle, I ought to be able to put off the rest of the report until we got to the fort.

"What did Ethan do?"

"Did he have one of his trials?"

"Are the Green Mountain Boys the ones who found out Benedict Arnold was a traitor?"

Dad patted my hand while the questions went on. "*Now* you can make them wait." He laughed.

While Mrs. Blair was getting our tickets I stood outside the little gate that led into the fort with everyone gathered around me.

"Ethan didn't want Benedict Arnold to lead the Green Mountain Boys into battle at Fort Ti," I began.

"Well, who would? He was a traitor," Peggy broke in before I could get any further.

"No, he wasn't!" I laughed, happy to have caught her in a mistake. "He wasn't a traitor until years later. At least, he *was* a traitor but only the way George Washington and Thomas Jefferson and every other colonist who took the Americans' side were traitors. If we hadn't won the war, all those people could have been hung by the British for fighting against them. You aren't supposed to attack your own government, and the British government was *our* government right up until the British gave up and said we won the Revolution.

"So," I concluded, "being a traitor had nothing to do with it."

I looked back at my paper.

"Ethan wanted to lead the Green Mountain Boys in the attack so that he would get credit for it. It wasn't just that he wanted the glory for himself, though that's nice, too. The Green Mountain Boys were the only militia in the Green Mountains, even if they weren't a legal one. Ethan hoped that if he and his militia helped to free the colonies from Great Britain, then the colonial government would support them in their fight against New York. If Arnold led the attack, it would seem as if they'd won because an outsider had helped them. Their claim wouldn't have been as strong, and Ethan wouldn't have had as much to bargain with.

"There could have been trouble over who was going to lead the attack except for one thing—Ethan had those three hundred Green Mountain Boys and Benedict Arnold had nobody. And those three hundred Green Mountain Boys took one look at Benedict Arnold and didn't like him. He thought they were just a bunch of poor farmers and that he was better than they were. Ethan was a farmer, just like them. He lived with them, he spoke for them, he was their kind of guy. Benedict Arnold wasn't. They told Arnold that they voted for their leaders, and they were sticking with Ethan. Some of them even said they'd go home if Arnold led the attack."

Mrs. Blair showed up with the tickets about then, which was perfect. I had just the thing to read before heading up the path toward the gate.

"One way or another, Ethan led them across the lake. Before they attacked he told his men, 'We must this morning either quit our pretensions to valour, or possess ourselves of this fortress in a few minutes; and, in as much as it is a desperate attempt (which none but the bravest of men dare undertake), I do not urge it on any contrary to his will. You that will undertake voluntarily, poise your firelocks.'

"Some people claim he just said, 'Let's go,' " I added. It seems much more likely to me.

"Let's go!" Jack shouted as the wooden gate opened.

"Valor," I whispered to Dad, repeating one of the words in old Ethan's speech. I figured people who can't read probably don't have very good vocabularies, and even I'd had to look the word up. I didn't want to risk him using it in some weird, wrong way in front of the others. "It means personal bravery."

"*Valeur,* of course. Does your old man look stupid?" Dad asked.

Actually, in those baggy pants and that light-colored jacket he looked like Ricky Ricardo back in the days when he still loved Lucy. I tried to keep my distance.

Fort Ticonderoga is built around a courtyard (which is actually called a Place of Arms, but who's ever heard of that?). The fort is supposed to look like a star, though you might have to be in a plane or something to see it. The rooms are all in this narrow strip of a stone building that is built around the courtyard. Outside this building is a steep embankment that leads down to the lake. To get into the courtyard, you have to go through this sort of tunnel built right into that strip of stone building that actually is the fort.

"This is where they went in," I explained, looking down at my papers as Mrs. Churchill began adjusting the dials and knobs on her camera. "There was a gate here then and a guard.

"The Green Mountain Boys were organized in three lines, with Ethan and Benedict Arnold in front of them. Ethan had told Arnold he could go with them, which seems like a nice thing to do but maybe he was hoping he'd get shot or something."

I could feel myself getting red as Mrs. Churchill's camera began to whir and she walked around me taking pictures of our group from different angles. No matter how hard I tried, I couldn't keep this jerky smile off my face.

"The guard shot at Ethan, but his gun misfired. Ethan ran at him, and the guard retreated through this archway into the courtyard, shouting to warn the others. Ethan followed with his troops behind him."

Mrs. Churchill ran ahead so she could get a picture of us coming through the archway. My face hurt so from grinning that it was hard to speak.

"Except for the guards, the British soldiers were still asleep. Ethan had his soldiers break up so some of them were facing the barracks that were on one side of the fort and some of them were facing the other. Then they started shouting, just to wake everyone up.

"A guard with a bayonet charged toward one of the Green Mountain Boys' officers. Ethan brought the flat of his sword down against the man's head. The guard dropped his gun and asked for quarter, which is what they called mercy back then.

"Ethan lowered his sword and asked him where his commanding officer stayed. The guard showed him some stairs leading up to a door in the second story. Ethan raced up them, shouting, 'Come out of there, you damned British rat!'

"An English officer came to the door wearing his coat. He had his pants draped over his arm. If I'd been him, I would have put on my pants and had my coat over my arm. If he had known he was going to go down in history as the officer who surrendered with his pants off, he probably would have been more careful how he dressed, too.

"He looked down across the courtyard to see that other officers of the Green Mountain Boys had ordered their men to break down doors. Ethan ordered him to hand over the fort to him.

" 'On whose authority do you demand it?' the officer asked. Which was probably a good question, seeing as he didn't even know he was at war with anybody.

" 'In the name of the great Jehovah and the Continental Congress,' Ethan replied. Jehovah is a fancy word for God. Ethan threw it in to his speech even though he wasn't much interested in religion, because he said he didn't think many people would know what the Continental Congress was, since it had only been running the country for a little while.

"Ethan sent one of his cousins (the Grants were crawling with his relatives) off with a hundred men to the fort at Crown Point, and they captured it the same day. The Green Mountain Boys, which was not a real army with real training, had taken control of the lake (and ninety gallons of rum stored at Fort Ti) from the British without losing a man or killing one. No casualties on either side!

"And Ethan, who was thrown out of one town and had to leave another so that legal charges against him would be dropped, became a hero all over the country."

I thought that was a good ending. I like when things happen in oral reports that are sort of the opposite of what you'd expect. Knowing what I know about Ethan Allen I sure wouldn't have expected him to become a hero.

"There's hope for everybody!" Pokie shouted after giving a cheer.

"Not everybody," Peggy sneered, looking at him.

"I didn't know they took control of the whole lake!" Wayne said, sounding impressed. "And without killing anybody!"

"And, remember, the other colonists lost when they fought the British at Lexington and Concord. *We* were the first ones to win," I reminded everyone.

"We were."

"We did it."

Dad, of course, totally missed the important part of the story and wanted to know about the ninety gallons of rum. "What did they do with it, them?" he asked.

"Well, actually, they drank it. They thought they should celebrate, you see," I admitted.

"You can do a lot of celebrating with that much rum," he said.

"We should celebrate, too," Jack suggested. "How about you let me have one of your cigarettes?" he said to Dad right in front of everyone.

"What's the matter with you? You don't know cigarettes stunt your growth, you?"

"Look at me," Jack replied, holding out his arms to make sure everyone could get a good view. "I need to have my growth stunted."

Dad gave him a light smack on the back of his head.

"Someone really needs to watch Jack," Mr. Santangelo whispered to Dad. "I noticed you seem to know him, and I was wondering if . . ."

"Know him! Why, I was best man at his parents' wedding! I remember when this boy was still in diapers. He was big like this then, too. And . . ."

"So you don't mind keeping track of him today?" Mr. Santangelo asked. I could tell he was trying to shut Dad up before the howling and laughing from the boys became deafening. Dad didn't even look embarrassed. But then, why should he? He never feels embarrassed. He just causes it in others.

So there I was, standing next to my father, while Jack

and the rest of the sixth-grade boys most likely to flunk out of high school were all jumping up and down around us, yelling that they wanted to look at guns. Parents are supposed to worry about their kids falling in with a bad crowd, they're not supposed to attract one themselves.

"Tessy! Tessy! Over here!"

I stood still and let Dad and the boys move off to a door to one side of the courtyard. That left me alone in that open space looking toward where Deborah and a group of girls were standing next to a short, squatty little cannon.

"I want to get a picture of my best friends," Deborah called.

I stood there for a second, sort of weak and stuck to the spot, which is the kind of feeling you'd usually expect when something awful happens. Then Mrs. Churchill signaled to me with one hand while she held that big camera of hers with the other and I ran over to join her.

"You get on one side of me and Yvette can be on the other," Deborah said while some of the other girls from the class stood gathered behind us.

I could hardly breathe as we all stood facing Mrs. Churchill, who kept telling us not to move while she held the camera up to her face and squinted into it. I had to concentrate on keeping my eyes open. I hate it when I see pictures of myself with my eyes closed. And I was worried that my blouse might be untucked and sticking out from under my sweater. I'm the only one that ever happens to.

I smiled and smiled all the time we were waiting for

Mrs. Churchill until I noticed Mrs. Blair with another group of girls. She was reading something to them, maybe that same brochure Mr. Santangelo had had, and everyone was looking at her except for Peggy. She was looking at us. I thought at first she was jealous, because that was what I would expect to be if I wasn't part of the best group at the field trip. Then I thought maybe she was angry, because that was what I would expect her to be because she wasn't part of the best group at the field trip. Then I thought she looked as if she were feeling sorry for us or me or someone in our group, though it was hard to tell because Peggy doesn't feel sorry for people very often. And why should Peggy feel sorry for me, was what I wanted to know. For once I was right where I wanted to be. Wouldn't you know Peggy would ruin it for me with a "you poor dumb thing" look. Wouldn't you just know . . .

The flash went off and the camera whirred. I was sure I wasn't looking as if I belonged in *Tiger Beat* or *16 Magazine*. But at least I was in the picture. I wish that Mrs. Churchill hadn't spoken French whenever she passed Dad and me. But at least she was talking to us. I wish that during lunch my father hadn't told everyone he had to see a man about a horse, which in his mind is a hilariously funny way of announcing a trip to the bathroom. But at least I was able to catch up with him to make sure that if he couldn't read the signs on the rest-room doors he wouldn't end up in the Ladies. I also wish that, when I showed him which bathroom to use, he hadn't said in a big loud voice,

"What's wrong with you?" But at least . . . well, there isn't an at least for that one.

All in all, it was not a bad day as my days go, I realized in the afternoon while I was leaning against the wall of the fort watching Mrs. Churchill take pictures.

Dad came up behind us and Mrs. Churchill spoke to him before taking a couple more pictures and hurrying off to the others.

"What did she say?" I asked.

"She hopes we leave soon because she and her husband are playing tennis tonight, and she has some things to do this afternoon," Dad said as he pulled his cigarettes out of his pocket. "Tell me if you see anyone coming, and I'll put this out, me," he continued as he lit up.

I leaned against the wall and sighed. "So Mr. Churchill plays tennis. That doesn't surprise me."

Dad nodded as he blew out his first cloud of smoke. "Tennis is for those sorts. Skiing, too. They don't work hard, them."

"He's got an important job," I argued.

"He sits at a desk," Dad said, the way he might say, "He eats out of the dog's dish."

I was about to leave and see if maybe I could hang around with Deborah so I'd end up sitting nearer her on the bus when Dad said, "You like telling stories, eh?"

I shrugged. "The Ethan Allen stories are the first ones I've ever told."

"You did a good job, you. The fancy lawyer's daughter,

she wasn't telling that story. That plumber's wife—" He stopped, and used the side of his finger to bang the bottom of his nose a couple of times as if he was pushing it up in the air. It's a little motion he often uses when he wants to show he's talking about a stuck-up snob. "Her girl wasn't telling any stories. *You* told the story." He held both his hands out toward me as he said "you." "*You* told it because *you* were the only one who knew how to tell it."

"Actually, I told it because my name was pulled out of a pencil holder," I admitted. "It was just dumb luck."

"Luck, she's not dumb. People say she's dumb because she doesn't always pick out the rich man or the man with the fancy job. That doesn't mean luck doesn't know what she's doing. She can still pick out the *right* man."

"I'm not a man, Dad."

"You know what I mean. Don't get picky with me about words, you. You'll ruin my train of thought."

No one has ever been able to ruin Dad's train of thought once it got going.

"Luck knew what she was doing when she picked you for this report. You finished it just right."

"Oh, I'm not finished," I said. "I'm just getting to the best part of the story."

TWELVE

"**M**rs. Ford's daughter had her baby," Peggy announced the next morning before classes started. "It was a boy."

"Oh-oh. Does that mean she's coming back?" Pokie asked. "She's only been gone a month." He looked both ways as if he expected Mrs. Ford to come sneaking up behind him.

"Soon. She has to wait for some other relative to arrive to help with—"

"We went on our field trip and finished the reports just in time then," Mr. Santangelo broke in. Thank goodness. What goes on in Mrs. Ford's daughter's house is pretty low on my list of interesting things, and Peggy sounded as if she could have gone on about it for quite some time.

"The reports aren't finished," I said to Mr. Santangelo.

"Oh? Who's left?"

"I am. The Ethan Allen report."

"But, Thérèse, how can there be more? You did the Battle at Fort Ticonderoga yesterday," Mr. Santangelo objected.

I felt a little flicker of nervousness. Was he going to say I couldn't read any more to the class? Was it all over?

"I'm beginning to feel a little guilty about how much work you've done, Thérèse. I think you've already done enough to earn your B."

I didn't know what to say. I knew Bs were few and far between and that I should just snatch that one up while I had the chance. But it had been two and a half weeks since I'd first stood up before the class and told those first stories about Ethan Allen. For two and a half weeks I'd been carefully piecing together facts and then hunting for—and finding—the exact word that would make people understand the elaborate Ethan Allen jigsaw puzzle I was putting together in my mind. And at some point during those two and a half weeks people had started to listen.

Two and a half weeks is a long time to be doing something and then suddenly have to stop. On the other hand, two and a half weeks isn't very long at all. You just can't get enough of people treating you like you're somebody in two and a half weeks to last you the rest of your life. I hadn't gotten enough to last me even to the end of the school year, and it was already the beginning of May.

I stood there, not knowing what to do, my mind full of thoughts about how if I could just read once more to the class, I'd be satisfied. I could go back to being just plain old Treesaw, the girl who was expected to say "boob" and say it often. Well, maybe I'd have to read two more times before I could do that. No. I'd better read three more times.

Would Mr. Santangelo let me write and read some extra-credit reports? Or how about if I wrote a real story and read that? Would that be okay? I had an idea for a story about a girl who was stolen by criminals and raised by them and . . .

"Does Tess have some more little-known facts to tell us about Ethan?" Wayne asked, sounding interested.

"I've got something better than little-known facts!" I answered instantly. "I've got Ethan. It's *his* report this time."

I looked over at Mr. Santangelo. "It's hard to explain. You'll understand."

"You've got Ethan?" Jack asked, looking kind of sly and crafty. "Does he swear and beat people up?"

"There is *more* to Ethan Allen than swearing and beating people up," I told him.

"But that's what I like about him. Let her give the report when we're supposed to have math," Jack suggested.

Math was among Jack's four or five worse subjects.

There was a lot of support for that idea and a lot of questions about what was going to be in the next part of the report. I didn't answer them, of course. You can ruin a good oral report by giving away too much.

"I'll tell you what," Mr. Santangelo said, sort of smiling. "Let's have Thérèse give her report right after lunch when we usually do our poetry talks."

His suggestion was greeted with a short round of applause and a couple of cheers. A few people started pounding their desks, and Jack jumped to his feet, looked up toward the ceiling with his arms raised, and shouted, "Thank you! Thank you!"

I liked that choice of time, too. Not that poetry bothers me any more than anything else we do at school, but waiting until after lunch gave me a few hours to work on finishing touches. I wanted to sort of punch things up. I took my books out of my desk and stacked them in front of me so that I could hide my papers behind them. Then I kept my head down, as if I were really, really interested in those word problems in my math book, and wrote away, adding some things, cutting out parts that were too long, and trying to make sure that I said enough to make everybody understood what was going on.

I brought the report with me to the cafeteria, which was a good thing. It gave me something to do, since there was no way I was eating that chipped beef in gravy on cold toast that the cook shoved at me. When I went outside for recess I still could think of things I wanted to change, so I sat down with my back against the school building and tried to squeeze notes into the margins of the paper.

"Guess what," someone said from above my head.

I squinted into the sun to see who had cast a shadow across my lap.

"What?" I said to Deborah.

"That's not guessing."

"I can't. I don't have time."

"I'm going to Yvette's this afternoon."

I just grunted and looked back at my papers.

"She's going to show me her barn."

"Hmmm."

"You have a barn."

I stopped what I was doing because I thought I'd heard a hint. Did Deborah want to come to my house? Deborah? In my bedroom? Looking at my stuff? That sure wouldn't take long.

"We're going to Yvette's barn to play with her kittens. Do you have kittens in your barn?"

"We've just got one cat that's missing a leg. It must have been a kitten once."

I wished she'd go away before I had to invite her over. We'd have a much better time at your place, I wanted to tell her. I would, anyway. I'd love to go back, especially if the invitation included dinner. Maybe her father would speak some Latin.

"Yvette and I are taking the school bus to her house, then my father is going to come pick me up when it's time for me to go home."

My head snapped up. "Your father?"

Deborah nodded. "He always picks me up."

If I didn't live on a farm, what would someone have to offer to make me want to visit one? I wondered. A lot. In fact, I didn't think there was anything anyone could offer that would make me step onto a farm if I didn't have to.

"The people who owned our farm before us kept horses in one of the barns. You can still see where the horses chewed on the wood on one side of a manger," I told Deborah, in a sort of "oh, by the way" tone of voice.

"Really?"

It didn't take long. Before you knew it, I was telling her that I would call her about a time when she could come visit the very spot where a horse used to live.

" 'Ethan Allen said that some of his many friends had really good reputations, which sounds to me as if some of his other friends didn't,' " was how I began the next portion of my report. I read as quickly as I could, mostly just because I can and there aren't that many things I can do well. But I also think that when something's read fast, it makes the people listening to it feel excited. Someone who is giving an oral report should do everything she can to make her listeners feel excited.

"Because those many friends, with good reputations and bad, insisted, he wrote a book. It wasn't about the 'battle of Ticonderoga,' which is what you'd think it would be about because the Americans thought that battle was a really big deal, it being the first battle they'd won—and won so easily, too. Instead, Ethan's story, his narrative, he kept calling it, was about what happened after the Continental Congress rewarded him for capturing Fort Ticonderoga by making him a real colonel. It was about what happened after Ethan wasn't an outlaw anymore, when he'd been a hero for three or four months.

"He figured that since conquering Ticonderoga had taken only a few hours, he would try to conquer something bigger, like Canada. To make a long story short so we can spend more time on what's going to happen later, Ethan led an attack on the city of Montreal. When he was with the Green Mountain Boys at Ticonderoga, everything went right. When he was with the colonial army at Montreal, everything went wrong. This time people did die, though Ethan wasn't one of them. Instead, at the end of September 1775—just four and a half months after his great victory at Ticonderoga—he was captured by the British."

I would have paused for effect then, but I'd let slip that Ethan was taken prisoner by the British long before, so what was the point?

" 'I handed an officer my sword,' Ethan said, 'and a half a minute later a savage advanced on me with more than mortal speed. At that instant I twitched the officer to whom I gave my sword between me and the savage, but he flew around me with great fury, trying to single me out to shoot me without killing the officer. I was nearly as nimble as he, though, keeping the officer in such a position that his danger was my defense. But in less than half a minute, I was attacked by just such another. Then I made the officer fly around with incredible speed. This went on for a few seconds when I saw a Canadian taking my part. And in an instant an Irishman came to my assistance, and drove away the fiends, swearing by Jasus he would kill them.'

" 'This tragic scene composed my mind. The escaping from so awful a death, made even imprisonment happy.' "

"That's Ethan speaking?" Wayne asked. "His own words?"

"All the good ones," I assured him.

Ethan could tell a good story, but he went on too long sometimes, if you ask me.

" 'I came to the barrack-yard at Montreal, where I met Gen. Prescott. He asked me whether I was that Col. Allen who took Ticonderoga. I told him I was the very man. Then he shook his cane over my head, calling many hard names and put himself in a great rage.

" 'I told him he would do well not to cane me, for I was not accustomed to it. Gen. Prescott ordered a sergeant's command with fixed bayonets to come forward and kill thirteen of the Canadians taken with me.

" 'It cut me to the heart to see the Canadians in so hard a case, as a result of their having been true to me. They were wringing their hands, saying their prayers (or so I concluded), and expected immediate death. I therefore stepped between the executioners and the Canadians, opened my clothes, and told Gen. Prescott to thrust his bayonets into my breast, for I was the sole cause of the Canadians taking up arms.

" 'My design was not to die but save the Canadians. The General stood a minute, then made the following reply: "I will not execute you now, but you shall grace a noose at Tyburn, God damn ye."

" 'I was a little inwardly pleased with his reply since it suggested to me the idea of postponing death, Tyburn being in England, not Canada.'

"Ethan spent the next six weeks in leg irons and handcuffs. He said he was 'obliged to throw out plenty of extravagant language'—I think we can guess what that means—which he said was useful at the time but he didn't think he needed to repeat it in his book.

"Once, 'upon being insulted, in a fit of anger I used my teeth to twist off a nail that went through the bar of my handcuff. At the same time, I swaggered over to those who abused me, particularly a Doctor Dace. I flung such a flood of language at him that it shocked him and the spectators, for my anger was very great. I heard one say, damn him, can he eat iron?' "

"They must have been sorry they ever captured him!" Pokie broke in eagerly.

"Eventually Ethan and about thirty-three other men who were captured with him were loaded onto another ship for the trip to England. They were all supposed to make the trip in one small room where they had to eat, sleep, and use two tubs for toilets for the entire trip.

" 'When I was first ordered to go into the filthy enclosure, I positively refused, and endeavored to reason with the captain. But all to no purpose, my men being forced in the den already, and the rascal who had the charge of the prisoners commanded me to go immediately in among the rest. He further added that the place was good enough for a rebel, that anything short of a noose was too good for me. A lieutenant said I should have been executed for my rebellion against New York and spit in my face. Upon which, though I was handcuffed, I sprang at him with both hands, and knocked him partly down. But he scrambled along into the cabin, and I after him. I challenged him to fight, and had the exalted pleasure to see the rascal tremble for fear. But the captain ordered the guard to get me into the place with the other prisoners dead or alive. Therefore, rather than die, I submitted to their indignities.

" 'We were denied fresh water, except a small allowance, and in consequence of the stench of the place, each of us was soon followed with a diarrhea and fever, which occasioned an intolerable thirst. When we asked for water, we were most commonly insulted; and to add to the horrors of the place, it was so dark that we could not see each other, and were overspread with body lice.' "

I had to pause to take a breath. I guess Jack thought I was done, because he yelled, "They went to the toilet in a tub!"

"Ethan called them 'excrement tubs.' I'll write it on the board," I offered, heading over toward the chalkboard.

"That's okay, Thérèse," Mr. Santangelo said. "That's not one of our spelling words this week."

"Okay. After about forty days, they arrived in England.

" 'When the prisoners were landed, multitudes of the citizens of Falmouth crowded together to see us, which was equally gratifying to us. The throng was so great, that the king's officers were obliged to draw their swords and force a passage to Pendennis castle, which was near a mile from the town, where we were closely confined.'

"They must have looked—and smelled—great. Ethan was wearing the clothes he'd had on when he was captured, and they hadn't been off him in the nearly six weeks that they were at sea!

"They were treated a lot better by the commander at the castle, who sent Ethan his meals and a bottle of wine a day. Ethan must have loved that. People would come to the castle every day to see the prisoners from America.

" 'Those that daily came in great numbers, out of curiosity to see me,' Ethan said, 'were united in this opinion, that I would be hanged. A gentleman from America who was friendly to me told me that bets were laid in London that I would be executed.'

"For months Ethan had been told he was going to be killed. What could he do about it? The only thing he had available to him was the trickery he had used against the New Yorkers all those years.

" 'I requested of the commander of the castle the privilege of writing to Congress. I wrote a short narrative of my ill treatment. But I carefully let them know that though I was treated as a criminal in England, it was all due to the orders of Gen. Carlton, who commanded the British in Canada. I asked that Congress not retaliate against the British prisoners it held until it learned how I, and the prisoners with me, were treated by the British in England. I addressed the letter "To the illustrious Continental Congress."

" 'The next day the officer from whom I obtained permission to write, came to see me and said, "Do you think that we are fools in England, and would send your letter to Congress, with instructions to retaliate on our own people? I have sent your letter to Lord North."

" 'This gave me inward satisfaction, for I found that the letter had gone to the identical person I designed it for, with a design to intimidate the English government and screen my neck from the noose. Nor do I know, to this day, but that it had the desired effect, though I have not heard any thing of the letter since.'

"At Christmastime Ethan and the other prisoners were suddenly taken from the castle, not to be hanged, but to be herded onto another ship for the trip back to America. Someone had gone to court and arranged for them to have their handcuffs taken off, so on this trip they had a little more freedom.

" 'When we were first brought on board,' Ethan

said, 'Captain Symonds ordered all the prisoners, and most of the hands to go on the deck, and caused to be read in their hearing certain rules. Then in a royal manner, he ordered the prisoners, me in particular, off the deck, and never to come on it again.

" ' "For," said he, "this is a place for gentlemen to walk."

" 'Prior to this I had taken cold, by which I was in an ill state of health and did not say much. However, two days after, I shaved and cleansed myself as well as I could and went on deck. The Captain spoke to me in a great rage, and said, "Did I not order you not to come on deck?"

" 'I answered him that at the same time he said, "That it was a place for gentlemen to walk" and that I was Col. Allen, but had not been properly introduced to him.

" 'He replied, "God damn you, Sir, be careful not to walk the same side of the deck that I do." '

"That's an exact quote from Ethan's book, just in case anyone wants to complain about my language again," I said, not mentioning anyone by name but meaning Mr. Santangelo or Peggy.

Mr. Santangelo just threw his hands in the air and said, "I'm not complaining."

" 'This gave encouragement and ever after that I walked in the manner he had directed, except when he at times ordered me off in a passion. Then I would directly afterwards go on again, telling him to command his slaves. I was a gentleman and had a right to walk the deck.' "

If I had been listening to that report, I would have wanted to know what made Ethan think he was a gentleman. But the others not only agreed that Ethan knew how to behave himself when he wanted to, they cheered when he said so. That "gave encouragement," as Ethan would say, so I went on.

"Ethan got sick while they were at sea. He had a little money and tried to buy some things from the ship's purser, who I guess runs some kind of store on ships. The captain wouldn't allow it.

" 'His answer to me, when I was sick, was that it was no matter how soon I was dead, and that he was in no way anxious to preserve the lives of rebels, but wished them all dead. I argued that the English government had acquitted me by sending me back a prisoner of war to America, and that they should treat me as such. I further suggested that it wasn't wise on their part to, by hard usage, destroy my life inasmuch as I might, if living, be traded for one of their officers. The captain replied that he needed no directions of mine how to treat a rebel, that the British should conquer the American rebels, hang the Congress and those who encouraged the rebellion (me in particular), and just retake their own prisoners. I gave him for an answer that if they waited till they conquered America before they hanged me *I should die of old age.*'

"Ethan reached North Carolina without dying. From there he was shipped with some other prisoners to Nova Scotia. He said the new captain was worse than the one he had just left. Captain Montague was, Ethan said, 'by nature underwitted.'

" 'In this passage the prisoners were infected with the scurvy, some more and some less, but most of them severely. The ships' crew was to a great degree troubled with it. I was weak and feeble as a result of so long and cruel a captivity, yet had but little of the scurvy.'

"Scurvy is a disease that's caused by not having enough vitamin C in your diet," I stopped to explain. "Sailors used to get it all the time because they didn't have any way of storing fruits and vegetables for a long trip at sea. Scurvy causes your gums to get soft and squishy and your teeth to get loose. After you've had it for a while you start to bleed under your skin so you can see dark spots where blood is collecting but can't get out of you. Your joints swell up and old scars open up again."

Scurvy is an interesting subject, I think.

" 'We arrived at Halifax not far from the middle of June. The prisoners were not permitted any sort of medicine, but were put on board a sloop which lay in the harbor and a guard constantly set over them. Here we were cruelly pinched with hunger.

" 'I sent letter after letter to Captain Montague,

who still had the care of us, but could obtain no answer. I wrote private letters to the doctors to procure some remedy for the sick, but in vain. The chief physician came by in a boat so close that the oars touched the sloop we were in, and I uttered my complaint in the genteelest manner to him, but he never so much as turned his head. I kept writing to the captain, till he ordered the guards, as they told me, not to bring any more letters from me to him.'

"Finally, the doctor who worked for the ship's captain snuck onto the prisoners' boat and gave Ethan a large bottle of drops. Ethan thought it saved the lives of several of the prisoners. Then one of the guards took pity on them and agreed to take a letter from Ethan to the governor of Halifax, who managed to get the sick prisoners into a hospital and the rest of them into another prison.

" 'There were about thirty-four of us who were all locked up in one common large room, and as sundry of them were infected with various illnesses the furniture of this spacious room consisted most principally of excrement tubs. I had not been more than three weeks in this place, before I lost all appetite to the most delicious food because of sickness. I grew weaker and weaker.'

"Somehow Ethan got the idea that eating raw onions would improve his health. I don't know where he got them, but eating them made him feel better. After four months in Halifax they were moved onto still another ship. This one was headed for New York.

" 'The Captain sent for me in particular to come on the quarter deck. I expected to meet the same rigorous usage I had commonly met with and prepared my mind accordingly. But when I came on deck, the Captain welcomed me to his ship, invited me to dine with him that day, and assured me that I should be treated as a gentleman. This was so sudden and unexpected a transition that it drew tears from my eyes (which all the ill usage I had before met with was not able to produce) nor . . .' "

"Stop!" Pokie shouted. "Make him say something funny! Make him swear at somebody! Don't make him cry!"

"But he did. He said so himself," I explained.

"This isn't what I thought it was going to be," Jack said very quietly . . . for him. "I thought . . . I thought it would be different. This should be more like *Hogan's Heroes*. Hogan never cries."

"I don't think I want to hear any more about people being sick, either," Deborah said. "It's not very nice."

"If they were sick, they were sick. Sickness isn't nice," Peggy said impatiently. She was leaning across her desk, watching me. "Go on," she ordered.

"He's going to be the old Ethan again," Wayne announced in that know-it-all voice of his I hate so. "Wait and see."

"Go on," a few voices repeated.

" '. . . nor could I at first hardly speak, but soon recovered myself and expressed my gratitude. And I let him know that I felt anxiety of mind in reflecting that his situation and mine was such that it was not probable that it would ever be in my power to return the favor. Captain Smith said this is a changeable world and one gentleman never knows but that it may be in his power to help another.

" 'Capt. Burk having been taken prisoner, was added to our company (he had commanded an American armed vessel) and was generously treated by the Captain and all the officers of the ship. We now had nearly thirty prisoners on board, and as we were sailing along the coast (if I recollect it right) off Rhode Island, Capt. Burk with an under officer of the ship came to our berth. He proposed to kill Capt. Smith and the principal officers of the frigate and take it, adding that there was £35,000 sterling on board. Capt. Burk urged me and the gentlemen that was with me to use our influence with the private prisoners to execute the design and take the ship with the cash into one of our own ports.

" 'Upon which I replied that we had been too well used on board to murder the officers; that I could by no means reconcile it to my conscience, and that in fact it should not be done. All the gentlemen in the berth opposed Captain Burk and his colleague. I then told them that they might depend upon it, upon my honor, that I would faithfully guard Captain Smith's life: if they should attempt the assault, I would assist him. Captain

Burk and his colleague went to stifle the matter among their associates.

" 'I could not help calling to mind what Captain Smith said to me when I first came on board: "This is a changeable world, and one gentleman never knows but that it may be in his power to help another." '

"They arrived in New York, and Ethan was finally paroled. But that didn't mean he was free. He wasn't allowed to leave the city. The British claimed he was crazy, but Ethan said he was no crazier than he'd ever been, though physically he was worn out from poor food and little exercise. He'd been a captive for fourteen months.

"An American fort on the Hudson River fell to the British just before Ethan arrived. Hundreds of private soldiers were brought to New York and crammed into churches.

" 'I have gone into the churches,' Ethan said, 'and seen sundry of the prisoners in the agonies of death, in consequence of hunger, and others speechless and near death, biting pieces of wood chips; others pleading for God's sake, for something to eat, and at the same time shivering with the cold. They would beg for God's sake for one copper, or morsel of bread. Hollow groans saluted my ears, and despair seemed to be imprinted on every of their countenances. The filth of these churches was almost beyond description. The floors were covered with excrements, I have carefully sought to direct my steps so as to avoid it, but could not. I have seen in one of these churches seven dead at the same time, lying among the excrements of their own body.

" 'The officers on parole were most of them anxious to give the miserable soldiers relief. But they had no means of buying the food the soldiers needed. The discussion of the officers was broken to pieces in consequence of the dread of offending Gen. Howe, who was responsible for the state of the prisoners. They were equally in his power with the soldiers.

" 'Mortality raged to such an intolerable degree among the prisoners, that the very school boys in the streets knew of it. At least they knew the prisoners were starved to death.'

"At the beginning of July 1777 Fort Ticonderoga fell to the British again. At the end of August, Ethan was taken into custody at the tavern where he was quartered and accused of breaking the terms of his parole.

" 'I now perceived myself to be again in substantial trouble.'

"He would be in substantial trouble for another eight months."

I looked over at Wayne and gave him a big smile as I sat down. *I* would decide if and when the old Ethan came back. "Why didn't the Green Mountain Boys go to New York and get him out of there?" Pokie demanded.

"That's right!" Jack agreed. "We wouldn't have let him rot in jail."

"What's next?"

"What happened to him?"

That's how you should leave your audience when you're doing an oral report—wanting more.

I told Mr. Santangelo that it looked as if I'd better do some more work on my report. He said, "Definitely."

THIRTEEN

My mother was kind of surprised that afternoon when I asked to have Deborah over. She couldn't believe that Deborah had hinted around that she wanted to come to our house. Not that Mom actually called me a liar or anything. She was just sort of shocked. On top of that, it had been a while since I'd invited a friend to our place. A long while. Years maybe. In fact, the last friend I'd had over had to go home early because he wet his pants.

Of course, it was Pokie, so maybe it wasn't that long ago.

What with being stunned and having to cook meals for Aunt Joséphine, who was on a special diet since that spell she'd had, and being worried about what Deborah would think of us (she did have a mother who wore earrings around the house, after all), it took Mom a day to work out a plan.

"Saturday," she announced at dinner Thursday night. "You and your father can pick her up after catechism class. Dad will bring you both home and pick up Marcel here so they can go take down Aunt Joséphine's storm windows."

Marcel dropped his fork on his plate with a clang. "What?" he yelled.

"But we'll have to use the truck because of the milk route," I objected.

Mom just looked at me as if she was daring me to complain so she could cancel the whole thing. I was too smart for her.

"I guess she'll have to eat with us, too, huh?" I said.

"I guess." Mom sighed.

"You know what I was thinking?" I asked.

"How unfair it is that I have to help take down Aunt Joséphine's storm windows and you don't?" Marcel suggested.

I ignored him. Aunt Joséphine has heavy wood-framed storm windows that fit over her regular ones, and after Marcel and Dad pry them off the house I usually have to wash them. I didn't want to draw our parents' attention to the fact that Mom's scheme left me out of that touching family custom.

"I was thinking," I said, answering my own question, "that it would be nice if our family started saying grace before meals."

Dad and Marcel looked at each other and shouted, "Grace!"

"Other families do it," I argued.

"We are not other families," Dad told me.

I'd noticed.

I was a little apologetic about making Deborah wait so long for my mother to make up her mind, but she acted as if she didn't think anything of it.

"It's going to be so much better going to your place on a Saturday instead of after school," she told me Friday morning. "When I was at Yvette's on Wednesday we saw their chickens and some of their cows, but we didn't get to spend hardly any time with their new calves. Tomorrow we'll have all afternoon so we won't miss a thing."

All afternoon? I thought. I had never spent that much time with someone who wasn't a relative in my whole life. We'd *have* to go see the chickens if we had to kill the whole afternoon. We'd *have* to visit each one separately.

"I love animals," Deborah sighed.

"Me, too," Jack shouted from where he was seated at his side of the circle of desks. "I especially love to eat them."

Deborah and some of the other girls squealed and made a fuss over that while I was walking over to my side of the room.

"She doesn't really like you, you know," a voice said behind me.

I turned around. Peggy had followed me. She was leaning toward me as if she thought that way we could have a private conversation while twenty-five other kids were in the room.

"Well . . . thanks for telling me" was all I could think of to say.

"I'm not just saying that to be mean," she went on, which was a good thing because it was exactly what I thought she was doing. "She doesn't really like me, either."

That certainly made sense.

"She's not as nice as everyone thinks she is," Peggy explained.

"Why are you telling me this stuff?" I asked.

"Because I'm nicer than everyone thinks I am," Peggy said, not sounding particularly nice if you ask me.

"You're trying to make trouble," I told her. "You're jealous because I'm friends with Deborah Churchill, and you're trying to ruin it for me."

It should have been a big ugly scene, but I had this great big smile on my face, what with being so happy that anyone at all was jealous of me, let alone Peggy Blair, and that kind of ruined the fight. What was Peggy supposed to say to that? Nothing. Which was just what she did say before she turned around and went off to join her own friends.

"So, Mr. Santangelo," I said, feeling confident that he was just sitting at his desk waiting to hear from me, "I have some more of my report ready. Shall I give it instead of that science lesson you were talking about yesterday?"

A little later, after everyone had put their science books away, I said,

"The Green Mountain Boys didn't go to New York to save Ethan, he didn't escape. He just stayed in jail until he was finally exchanged for a British prisoner thirty-two months after he was first captured in Montreal. No other American officer would be imprisoned as long during the Revolution. Whether he was in the company of prisoners or gentlemen, 'I was the same man still,' Ethan said. He never changed. It was just the way he was viewed by the people around him that was different.

"After he was released, Ethan was taken to Valley Forge, where he met George Washington, who said afterward, 'There is an original something in him that commands admiration.'

"What exactly that something was ol' George couldn't say.

"Ethan then 'set out for Bennington, the capital of the Green Mountain Boys,' as he called it, 'where I arrived the evening of the last day of May to their great surprise; for I was to them as one rose from the dead.'

"It must have seemed that way to Ethan, too. As leader of the Green Mountain Boys, he had won the first battle of the Revolution. While he was in prison, his cousin led the Green Mountain Boys and saved the day at the Battle of Bennington—and he did it without Ethan. As the spokesman for the Grantsmen, Ethan had led the fight against the New Yorkers who wanted to take their land. While he was in prison, the Grantsmen declared the area where they lived a state—and they did it without Ethan. Ethan had written all those pamphlets and newspaper articles arguing that the poor farmers in the Green Mountains had a right to their land. While he was in prison, those poor farmers wrote the first constitution stating that no one could be enslaved—and they did it without Ethan.

"For Ethan it must have been like dying and coming back in the future. His home wasn't even in the same place. Bennington had been in the New Hampshire Grants. The New Hampshire Grants were the only place Ethan had ever lived where people liked him and he could fit in. He came out of prison and found the Grants didn't exist anymore. Now Bennington was in Vermont. Ethan was nobody again.

"Until he wrote that book I told you about, *A Narrative of Colonel Ethan Allen's Captivity*. He told about his adventures traveling back and forth to England, how badly the enemy had treated him and the other prisoners, and how the British were starving our soldiers who were being held in those churches in New York. Well, everybody loves to read that kind of thing."

"That's right," Pokie broke in. "And he had all that stuff about people getting sick, too."

"And the toilet tubs," Jack reminded him.

"The book was so popular and sold so well that the publisher had to print copies eight times in two years. Which has to make you wonder if those people in Massachusetts and Connecticut who didn't want him living in their towns back when he was young and always in trouble read it. What did *they* think when

Ethan's *Narrative* made the colonists want to go on fighting the British? What did they think when it made Ethan a hero again? What did they think when they realized Ethan was someone others listened to?

"Once, a couple of years after he got back from prison, two little girls—really little—got lost in the woods near Ethan's home. People from all around came to help look for them. They hunted for three days. When it started to get dark on that third day, the search party was ready to give up.

"But Ethan was there. And he told those people that they should all think of those little girls as their own little girls, and they should feel the same pain and fear that their parents felt. And then he asked them if they could really give up and go home without making one more try to find those children, who might at that very moment be sobbing for their parents to rescue them.

"Grown men stood there and cried while they listened to Ethan. Then they went out one more time. And they saved those little girls."

That might be my favorite Ethan Allen story, though I like the one about riding into New York and having a drink at a tavern while there was a price on his head, too. The story about tricking the two New Yorkers into thinking he'd hung their partners during the night isn't bad, either. And any story where Ethan swears at a minister or a judge is bound to be a good one. But to be able to think of the words that will make people feel what you want them to feel, to be able to say them in a way that will make people do what you want them to do . . . Well, other people can think what they please, but me, I say it's hard to beat the "Tale of the Lost Girls."

"Those girls' father would never allow anyone to say anything bad about Ethan, even though we all know there was plenty that was bad to say.

"Even so, Vermont made him a general and asked him to head its militia. It makes perfect sense that he would accept the job because Vermont was a mess back then, and Ethan was always attracted to trouble.

"You see, after the Green Mountain Boys won the first battle of the American Revolution for the colonists back at Ticonderoga in 1776, the Grantsmen turned to Congress for help in their land fight with New York. Not only did Congress refuse to help, it said we should submit to New York. The people in Congress talked a lot about fighting the Revolution for freedom and liberty and all that, but they really wanted freedom and liberty just for the people who were running the colonies right then. As far as Congress was concerned, there were thirteen colonies, including New York, and its job was to look out for the rights of those thirteen colonies. In order to help a bunch of poor, powerless farmers in the Green Mountains, Congress would have had to ignore New York's claims to Vermont. It refused to do that.

"But we wouldn't give in. Instead, we decided it should be up to us to choose how we'd be governed. So we wrote a constitution, called ourselves Vermont, and told Congress we no longer wanted it to help us. Instead, we wanted it to let us become a state. By that time, we had been supporting the American cause in the Revolution for two years. Our men, Ethan among them, had fought with the Continental army and with the Green Mountain Boys. The year before Ethan was released from prison, Congress thanked us for all we had done by saying we just did not exist. But we did exist, and we continued to exist—separately from the rest of the colonies, as the Republic of Vermont."

"How could they ignore Congress?" Deborah asked. "That doesn't seem right."

"Congress was ignoring us," Peggy told her.

"But it was *Congress*. That's the top of our government," Deborah repeated. "You have to listen to Congress."

"If we had listened to Congress we'd have had to let New York govern us. And New York wanted to take our land away from us," I reminded her.

"Congress was breaking that unwritten law about not taking the liberty and property of another. How could we agree to let them do that to us?" Wayne asked.

It's scary the way he remembers everything he hears. It kind of makes me want to be careful about what I say in front of him.

"Well, we *didn't* let them do that to us," I said, trying to get back to the report. "Instead, we continued on as a separate country."

"My own country," Jack said. "I've always thought I should have one."

I bet a lot of people would agree with that.

"One thing that hadn't changed while Ethan was in prison was that his home, which was now the Republic of Vermont, was still caught right between the American colonies and Canada, which was British. And Britain and America were still at war. Britain was his enemy, but America sure wasn't doing anything to help him out. Congress wouldn't send Vermont ammunition for its militia when we asked for it, even though we were fighting their war for them! Once Ethan was head of the Vermont militia, he had to go to Connecticut and buy ammunition for us. He had to promise to pay for it himself.

"So there Ethan is, head of the militia in a spot where the militia may have to protect the public from invasion from Britain to the north and getting absolutely no help from the Americans to the south. And, of course, the Americans to the west are New Yorkers, so you can just imagine how they much *they* want to help us out.

"Well, perhaps you all remember that Ethan didn't have a very good reputation. Before the war he was a wanted man in New York. He used terrible language. He had all kinds of complaints about ministers and churches. He hung around in taverns. He hadn't made a very good impression on the British while he was a prisoner. Lots of people didn't like him and were willing to say so. The British got the idea that he was a person with no sense of honor. On top of all that, it was well known that Ethan and the other Vermonters weren't getting along with Congress. The British commander in Canada contacted him and offered to give Vermont everything it wanted if it would come over to the British side in the war. They tried to bribe Ethan, just as the New Yorkers had years before."

I stopped and didn't say anything for a few seconds. It's good, when you're giving a report, to give everybody a chance to sort of mull things over every now and then.

"So did he do it?" Pokie finally asked.

"Of course he didn't, you idiot. We're Americans, aren't we?" Peggy told him.

"Besides, nobody would be giving a big oral report on him if he was a traitor," Wayne pointed out.

"Tess would," someone said, and everybody laughed.

"Why would he be a traitor?" I asked. "We had offered to join the United States, but Congress said no. Congress may have thought we belonged to New York and were part of America, but we didn't think we belonged to anybody. We weren't part of anything. Shouldn't we have been able to do whatever we wanted?

"Ethan had set up garrisons and moved women and children to safer areas in the southern part of the state.

He was prepared for a British invasion, but he didn't want it to happen. When Britain made its offer to allow Vermont to join the Commonwealth as an independent country, Ethan didn't say no. After all, why would Britain invade Vermont if it thought it had a chance of making it an ally without firing a shot?"

"So he tricked them!" Wayne broke in. "He let Britain think he would give it what it wanted so it wouldn't invade Vermont."

I should have been mad at him. If oral reports had punch lines the way jokes do, he had just stolen mine. But I knew something he didn't.

"You probably all remember the letter Ethan wrote to Congress from the castle in England where he was imprisoned. Its purpose was to trick the British into keeping him alive. He did the same kind of thing for the next three years, only this time he was trying to trick Britain *and* Congress—Britain into not attacking Vermont and Congress into accepting Vermont as a state. He talked with Britain, and he let Congress know, through messages from Vermont's governor, letters, and rumor, that Britain would let Vermont live independently of New York even if Congress wouldn't.

"The war ended in 1783 without Vermont being attacked by the British. But Vermont still wasn't part of the Union. We thought we were an independent republic, though Congress still wanted us to be part of New York. We were willing to become a state, but Congress didn't want any states that hadn't been colonies. Even though it had just fought a war to separate from Britain, the charters from the king, which had created the colonies in the first place, were—to the members of Congress—what gave the thirteen original states their right to exist. It wasn't interested in forming new states just because citizens wanted them. That was more democracy than Congress could stand.

"But the war with Britain *was* over, and Vermont, as far as Ethan was concerned, was up and running no matter what Congress thought. Though it wouldn't be admitted to the Union until 1791, Ethan turned his attention to something else."

"Aren't you going to tell us?" someone called out as I sat down.

"What did he turn his attention to?"

"There's something we've hardly talked about at all," I explained.

"Make her tell us now, Mr. Santangelo," Peggy demanded. "I hate to be left hanging."

"You're going to like it," I promised her.

"You've done a very good job, Thérèse," Mr. Santangelo told me. "You don't need to do any more if you don't want to."

"But I do."

He gave me such a big smile I thought his face was going to pop. "Didn't I say any student could do well?" he asked everyone.

Monday would be the last day, I thought as Mr. Santangelo told everyone that they could learn a lesson from me, and he expected the same kind of high-quality work from everyone in the room. But that was going to be okay. I was ready.

And the ending was going to be such a surprise. Everyone was going to love it.

FOURTEEN

*E*vidently my father never washes the windows in his truck. Once I started thinking about it I realized I'd never seen him do it, and he'd never made Marcel or me do it, either. But I'd never noticed until I was in the cab, crammed between Dad and Deborah. I turned to speak to her and there was her profile against the window, which looked as if it was caked with something awful. But, really, I'm sure it was just dirty.

It had never bothered me that I couldn't put my feet flat on the floor when I was riding in the truck, either. There's a pair of cables for jump-starting batteries down there, and you sort of just have to prop your feet on them. But Deborah noticed. I could tell by the way her eyes flickered that she noticed all the old cigarette butts on the floor, too. And if she noticed that, you can be sure she noticed that the upholstery on the seat was gone and had been replaced with an old blanket.

How could she miss it?

"We got a letter yesterday from my camp. I've been accepted for two weeks in July," Deborah announced after we finished discussing how I'd never won anything at catechism class while she had received a pin every year for memorizing Bible verses at Sunday school. "When are you going?"

"To camp?" I laughed. "Only rich kids go to camp!"

"Peggy goes, and she's not rich. Her father's just a plumber."

I felt my own father twitch next to me.

"Peggy goes to 4-H camp," I said. That made me think of the story of how my mother got into a fight with Mrs. Blair over pom-poms during a 4-H meeting and told her what she could do with them. So, of course, I had to tell it.

"She really told her that?" Deborah whispered to me while Dad laughed.

Deborah doesn't look quite so pretty when her eyes are popping out of her head.

And she was really stuck on the subject of summer camp. "You'd love my camp," she said to me after she'd recovered some. "It's on a lake in Massachusetts. My friends and I have been going there for years. Yvette applied to go one of the weeks while I'm there. It's only a little over a hundred dollars a week if you don't take horseback riding lessons."

I could feel my father's body start to twitch again.

"It's too late for you to get in this summer, but you could try for next year," Deborah suggested.

Yeah, I thought. And I could try for a trip to the moon next summer, too.

It was only ten-thirty when we got home.

It was ten-forty when we finished looking at my bed, bureau, and the wooden broom handle that had been stuck into the walls in one corner of my room to make a clothes bar for my three or four dresses, a couple of blouses, and my coat.

"There are no closets in the entire house," I explained. Then I had to make an excuse for the wallpaper, which was printed with enormous purple peonies on a gray background and was attracting Deborah's attention. "There were only five prints in my mother's price range. You should have seen the other four."

"My mother is always doing that kind of thing," Deborah said, shaking her head in disgust. "She is always going on about how I have to learn the value of money. This spring she made me buy a whole bunch of skirts and blouses so I can mix and match them and get more wear out of my things. You can be sure she gets whatever she wants, though.

"Come on, let's canter down to the barn," Deborah said at ten-fifty after we'd left the house, having finished looking at everything in it. She took off with this weird step-pause movement that made her knees come up in front of her and looked goofy as all get out. Even though I was sure Dad and Marcel were gone and Mom was inside rolling out pie dough, I couldn't bring myself to do more than lift my right knee up a couple of times, which just made me move sideways.

"Isn't this too bad," Deborah said when I showed her the barn with the chewed-up manger.

"Yeah. The poor horse must have been hungry to be trying to eat wood," I agreed as we gazed at the front of a wooden trough that had been built onto a wall. The top of it was no longer straight, but worn down in the middle.

"Not that. They just chew at things. I meant all the box stalls have been torn out. It looks as if there were four. This was a real horse barn once."

"Dad tore out the stalls so cows he's not milking can come in here in the winter to get out of the cold."

"You could have had a stable, Tessy. Instead . . ." Deborah looked around at the mangers Dad had built along the opposite wall so that there would be hay put out on both sides of the barn at the same time.

"The idea was that the heifers would come in whenever they wanted and they would all have room to get to food and eat," I explained. I thought it would look bad if I didn't point out that, though he was an idiot, my father had at least meant well.

"The Morrissettes don't have a real horse barn," Deborah told me. "Even one like this. I bet you could fix this one up, if you wanted to."

I had been feeling what little interest I had in horses dribbling away over the last week or so, and my father had never had any at all. I said I didn't think it was likely the barn would ever hold anything but cows again.

Evidently, Deborah didn't care as much for cows as she did horses, because when one poked its head into the barn I was able to get her out of there. We went on to the hay barn, where things went a lot better. There wasn't much hay left because it was so close to summer, so we piled up the bales we could find to make houses. If we hadn't found the mice, we probably would have stayed there a lot longer.

"I thought you said you had a cat," Deborah complained after she'd screamed and run around for a while. "Aren't cats supposed to catch mice?"

"Gimpy does catch mice. But he doesn't have many teeth left, and all he can do is gum them and let them go."

Deborah said something like "Oh, gross" as she disappeared out the barn door.

"So what do you want to do next?" I asked, hoping we wouldn't have to go down to the chicken house before lunch. That would leave us with absolutely nothing to do in the afternoon.

"We could listen to music," Deborah suggested. She sort of sighed as she said it, as if she was getting worn out, but I think she was probably bored. I was.

"I suppose we could take the kitchen radio to my bedroom. Who knows? Maybe we'll be able to pick up more than three or four stations in there," I said, not very enthusiastically. I would have offered to move the family record player into my bedroom, but we didn't have one.

I was thinking of ways we could try to hitch up clothes hangers and aluminum foil to the old clock radio, when we got into the kitchen.

"Poutine!" I exclaimed when I saw what Mom was dishing out onto plates. "Where did it come from?"

"Where does all the food around here come from? I made it," Mom explained.

"Ah . . . what is this called again?" Deborah asked as she watched Mom ladle thick brown gravy out of a pan on the stove.

"Poutine. We have it all the time when we go to visit relatives in Canada," I said, trying to hide the fact that I was speaking with my mouth full.

"But what is it? I recognize the gravy, and I recognize the French fries. But what's that in between them?"

"Cheese." I carefully picked up a big piece of it with my fork and placed it in my mouth. "Ahh. You can hear it squeak when you chew it."

"Are you sure you should be eating that? It looks as if it's gone bad. Maybe that's why it squeaks."

"It squeaks because it's cheese curds. You know how when they make cheese there's a point between the time the milk curdles and the point when everything gets pressed into a block?" Mom asked.

"No," Deborah said as she slowly sat down next to the plate Mom had placed in front of her.

"Well, that's when you get cheese curds," Mom told her. "They're fantastic, and you can't get them around here. One of Mr. LeClerc's uncles came down from Canada yesterday and brought these with him." Mom looked at me. "Dad stopped at Mémé's while you were in catechism class to get them. He had them in the back of the truck so you'd be surprised."

"Oh, I am! I am!" I assured her as I carefully separated a few cheese curds that hadn't been covered with gravy from the rest of the food so I could eat them separately later. Then I cut up some fries and swirled them around to make sure they got covered with everything.

"Thanks, Mom."

"You're welcome, sweetie." Mom tossed back a couple of curds from a little bowl she had next to her and went to work beating some cream in a big mixing bowl.

"What's the cream for?" I asked. "You didn't make tarte au sucre, did you? You did? Deborah! We're getting sugar pie for dessert!"

Deborah stared at me with her mouth open. "A pie made of sugar?"

"Well, it has a crust, too," Mom admitted. "And, of course, there'll be whipped cream on it."

I couldn't believe it. If I had *asked* Mom to make even one of those things for a friend, she would have said something like "Who are you having over? The pope?"

"She only makes tart au sucre at Christmas!" I explained to Deborah.

Deborah made a noise to indicate she'd heard me. She was too busy picking at the French fries at the edge of her plate to carry on a conversation.

I could see her poutine beginning to congeal—the brown gravy was beginning to form a thin skin and the melted cheese curds were thickening. Soon the best moment for eating it would have passed.

"You're not going to leave that, are you?" I asked, horrified.

Deborah looked up. "N . . . no," she said. "I'm eating. See? . . . I've eaten all this part. I . . . uh . . . don't know if I'll be able to finish it, though. I had *such* a big breakfast."

"Give me that," I ordered, snatching her plate out from under her fork.

"Oh, no, you don't," Mom said, grabbing hold of the other side of the plate. "You've got your own."

"But mine's almost gone!" I told her.

Mom started laughing. "I haven't had any yet."

"You've had a whole bowl of cheese curds! I saw you eating them!"

"It was a little bowl," Mom said. "And there was no gravy on them."

"So put some gravy on them!"

"But then I still wouldn't have French fries. I didn't make any extra because they're no good cold."

Mom was reaching for a fork from the drawer in the cabinet without letting go of the plate, which meant, since I wasn't letting go, either, that I had to stretch across the table to hold on.

"Got it!" Mom exclaimed as she held up a fork. "I'll race you to the middle," she offered, and we both dug in, while I was still lying across the kitchen table.

"Ummm," Mom said after her first . . . or second . . . or third . . . mouthful. "It's like pudding."

"With lumps," I agreed.

Deborah had pulled away from the table, probably when I ended up on top of it, and after a while we realized she was staring at us.

"You sure you don't want to try some?" Mom asked. "There are lots more curds and gravy."

Deborah shook her head.

The best thing that could be said about lunch was that there was plenty of leftovers for later. It gave me something to look forward to during the long hour or two we were out picking wildflowers that afternoon.

We headed down to the woods by way of the fenced-in lane the cows use, passing small groves of trees that grew along fence lines dividing one meadow from another. The lane opened up into the big pasture. It was too hilly to try to bring a tractor and bailer into and broken up here and there by large outcroppings of rocks filled with crevices from which all kinds of things grew.

"Here's where we come with our sleds in the winter," I said as we stood at the top of a hill that sloped slowly down to a flat area that was bordered, on the far side, by a thick growth of trees we couldn't see beyond.

"Look at the size of it!" Deborah exclaimed because, in addition to being a long hill, it was wide. "What a great place to go tobogganing."

"We don't have a toboggan—just a couple of old wooden sleds with metal runners." Rusty metal runners, though I didn't think it was necessary to go into detail.

"I have a toboggan. So does Greg. You and I could give

a sledding party here next winter," Deborah suggested, grabbing hold of one of my arms.

I laughed. "Who would come?"

"Yvette. Tammy. Lynn and Peggy . . . everybody."

Everybody. "It is a good hill, isn't it?"

"We could have a fire at the top so everyone can warm up," Deborah went on, "and—"

"Marshmallows," I broke in, grabbing her arm now. "We can all roast marshmallows!"

"And how about hot chocolate! We can have hot chocolate!"

"Sure! The one thing we have a lot of is milk!" I laughed.

We ran down the hill a few times (we didn't dare roll down—it was a pasture used every day by twenty-five cows, after all) to sort of try out the slope and even collected some sticks from the edge of the woods to mark out sledding trails.

"Maybe we could do it during Christmas vacation," Deborah said as we headed back toward the barn. She had taken off her sweater to fill it with Dutchman's britches and adder's tongues. I was carrying a big fistful of stinkpots for the two of us to split since she didn't want anything that smelled that bad on her clothes.

I gasped. "If we do that, maybe we can cut an evergreen tree in the woods and put it up on the hill and decorate it!"

"That's a great idea!"

We came out into our driveway near the fenced-in barnyard. We could see Mr. Churchill waiting for us next to the house. He and Dad were leaning against the Churchills' station wagon, their arms crossed, looking as if they didn't have much to say to each other.

"Gee, your father even wears a suit on Saturday," I said admiringly.

"He has to," Deborah confided. "He looks weird when he wears normal clothes. What was that?" she gasped as something black went whizzing along the ground not far from our feet.

"Gimpy. Isn't it incredible how fast he can run on just three legs?"

Without even thinking about it, I turned to see what was after that old cat that could make him move like that. So that was how I happened to see the big bony dog coming around the barn, his hair all different shades of brown and all different lengths, his winter coat hanging around him in chunks.

"Brownie!" I shouted, thinking Deborah would understand the warning. I turned and ran toward the only protection I could see, the barnyard fence.

I heard the men shouting behind me and turned around. Deborah was right where I'd left her, with her father heading down the driveway toward us, his suit jacket flapping behind him. Brownie, of course, hadn't slowed down for even a second.

"Run!" I shouted at Deborah's back. "Run."

I was just heading back toward her when she finally decided Brownie was as close as she wanted him to get. She dropped her sweater and started moving toward me.

We would never have made it to the fence if Brownie hadn't noticed Mr. Churchill. The dog paused to look from us to Deborah's father as if he was trying to make a choice from a menu. As usual, he was growling with his mouth open. I don't think I ever saw that animal when he wasn't showing off every tooth in his head. Mr. Churchill was clearly impressed because he stopped dead in his tracks and even looked as if he was getting ready to take off in some other direction.

"Do something, Daddy!" Deborah wailed. "Help me!"

Mr. Churchill looked as if he was going to cry. His glasses were crooked and he just stood there looking from the dog to Deborah. He raised his arms in a confused shrug. It didn't look to me as if there was much help coming from there. I struggled up to the top rail of the fence and tried to pull Deborah up after me.

That was when Brownie made his decision. He was going for young, tender meat.

"Deborah!" Mr. Churchill shouted, his arms stretched out before him as if he was going to try to hug her one last time. Deborah screamed, and I closed my eyes, wondering if I was going to be knocked over backward into the muck of the barnyard or ripped up where I sat and left dangling like those woodchucks that are shot and thrown over barbed-wire fences.

There was a terrible yelp that I thought must be Deborah since I knew it wasn't me. Then there was another, accompanied by a thud. That was followed by whimpering, grunts, and a chopping or banging noise.

Deborah was still next to me, screaming away, when I opened my eyes.

"Damn!" I said, when I saw what was on the ground in front of me.

Brownie was lying there, not exactly in pieces, but chopped up badly enough to have sent blood and gore in every direction. Standing over him, a shovel held high over his shoulder ready to strike again, was my father.

"Daddy!" Deborah sobbed.

Mr. Churchill hurried over and helped her down from the fence. Once Deborah was on the ground, closer to the death scene, she started screaming all over again.

"Stop that," Mr. Churchill said, shaking her. "You're not hurt. Calm down."

Deborah quieted down some but not enough. Mr. Churchill tried to get away from her long enough to help me down, but she clung to him and whined something that sounded an awful lot like "dead doggy" to me. Otherwise, he would have reached up and maybe taken my arm so I wouldn't lose my balance. I hope he wouldn't have tried to lift me. That would have been embarrassing all the way around. But nothing like that happened because Deborah whimpered and shook and took all Mr. Churchill's attention for herself. I had to get off that fence and back onto my feet on my own.

"Dad," I said, my own voice trembling a bit, "Mr. La-Fontaine said he'd call the police if you killed his dog."

Dad had pounded the tip of the shovel into the ground so it would stand up by itself. He was trying to light a cigarette, but his hands were shaking. He finally dropped the match and spit out the cigarette so they both ended up in the blood on the ground.

Mr. Churchill handed Dad a small white business card. "If the dog's owner gives you any trouble about this, call me right away. I'll take care of that for you."

Dad nodded and slid the card into the breast pocket of his flannel shirt.

"Can I help you . . . with this?" Mr. Churchill asked, waving his hand at the mess on the ground.

"No. No," Dad replied. "You're not dressed for this kind of work, you."

Mr. Churchill looked down at his pants, which were covered with spots down by his shoes. "I suppose not," he said.

As I watched Mr. Churchill leading Deborah, who was still sobbing in a nice gentle way, to their car, Marcel came out of the house to find out what was going on. He took one look at the dog and shouted some things that should only be said in church.

"We could bury him," he suggested after he heard what had happened.

Dad shook his head. "The man has to know, him, what became of his dog. Go get a couple of grain sacks from the barn."

Marcel ran off for the grain sacks while I watched Dad try to light another cigarette with more success. He blew out a cloud of smoke and stared off into space, his eyes narrow, thinking.

It was Dad who used the shovel to get Brownie onto one of the feed bags while Marcel kept giving directions like, "Watch it, you're missing some." I used another bag to cover Brownie up. Dad and Marcel each took an end of the burlap shroud and carried the body to the back of the truck.

I was afraid Mr. LaFontaine wouldn't be home and we'd be stuck driving around with a dog's body for hours or even days. Or maybe he would have company. What if his grandchildren were visiting and there we would be with a dead dog?

None of that could have been much worse than what actually happened. Dad brought the old man out to the back of the truck. He lifted the top bag off from Brownie's body, and Mr. LaFontaine began to cry.

"Oh, Monsieur Brun, Monsieur Brun," he babbled as he took a big red handkerchief out of his pocket and wiped his face. Marcel and I hung back a little, a lot more shaken then we would have been if Mr. LaFontaine had started in swearing and yelling the way we'd expected him to.

Finally, he dried off his face, sniffed a few times, and turned a hard look on my father. "You killed my dog, you."

"*Je regrette*, François," Dad said, giving a big shrug. "But the little girl he attacked . . . her father, he's a lawyer, him. I had to do something. A lawyer! That one gets you in court, you could never get out."

"A lawyer?"

"From New Jersey."

Mr. LaFontaine gasped.

"Are you sure he's a lawyer, Dad?" Marcel asked from beside me. I reached behind him and pinched the back of his thigh, trying to shut him up. He twisted away from me and said, between gritted teeth, "I heard at school that he's a judge."

"A judge!" Mr. LaFontaine cried, throwing up his hands.

Dad held up his hand with his finger and thumb close together. "You came this close to losing everything you have, you," he said. "Judges."

Dad spat on the ground, something that usually grosses me out but seemed just the right thing to do then.

Mr. LaFontaine shook Dad's hand and thanked him over and over while Marcel and I got stuck unloading Brownie from the back of the truck.

"If a poor man won't help a poor man, who will?" Dad asked.

"If there's anything I can do for you, Roland, you remember me, eh?" Mr. LaFontaine called as we started to roll out of his driveway.

We sat in a straight sober line, Dad behind the wheel, me in the middle, and Marcel next to the door, until we were out of sight of Mr. LaFontaine's farm. Then we began to laugh so hard Dad had to pull over until we could sit up straight again and wipe our eyes.

FIFTEEN

The events of the weekend pretty much put every other thought out of my mind. Even on Monday morning I was kept busy on the bus telling everyone about how I'd survived a dog attack. I don't spend a lot of time thinking about what's going on at school, anyway, but I never gave it a thought that day. So I was totally unprepared to walk into class and find our desks in rows. Everyone suddenly became quiet. We silently tiptoed into the classroom and sat down, the way you do when you go to a funeral home for a wake. Except that at the front of the room, instead of a coffin, there was Mrs. Ford.

She did not look happy to be back.

"Peggy, you may put the date on the board for us, please," Mrs. Ford announced.

Peggy looked as if she'd expected something far worse and was relieved to have been asked to do such a normal thing. She was encouraged enough to stop at Mrs. Ford's desk when she was done.

"Where is Mr. Santangelo?" she asked.

"At home, I assume."

"We didn't know he was leaving so soon. My mother and I thought it would be nice to give him a party."

"He won't be coming back," Mrs. Ford said without looking up.

That was followed by a silence so long Jack wordlessly indicated to a couple of the others that he was about to liven things up by sticking his hand under one of his armpits so he could make a nice, loud, rude noise. His arm dropped down when Mrs. Ford suddenly announced, "We're going to spend today getting back into our routine and trying to catch up on everything you haven't done this past month. Yes, Theresa?"

"If we're going to be back in our routine soon, maybe I should finish my Ethan Allen report today," I suggested.

Mrs. Ford's mouth dropped. "*You* gave the Ethan Allen report?"

I could see heads flipping back and forth as the other kids in the room watched to see what was going to happen.

"Yes, I did," I said. I couldn't wait for her to hear what I'd written.

Mrs. Ford slammed a stack of papers down on her desk. "I don't see why I can't take care of a family emergency without everything falling apart here. I get no support at all."

She slammed some drawers and shuffled things and sighed as if she had to clean up after someone who was really sloppy. Which she did, since neatness was another thing like calendars that Mr. Santangelo believed kept him from being creative.

"You're late, Theresa. Those oral reports should have

been done by now. Is there anyone else who hasn't given their report?" Mrs. Ford asked.

If there was anyone else left with a report to give, he or she decided to take a zero rather than admit it.

"Okay. Get up here," Mrs. Ford said. She shoved her chair back, crossed her arms, and stared at me.

I brought the whole report up with me, every page I'd written. "I'm not late, Mrs. Ford. It's a long report," I explained, showing it to her. I had never done anything that big before.

"You're not going to read all that, are you?" she asked, sounding horrified.

"I've already read most of it. I just have to finish."

"Then do it."

"In 1783 the war ended and Ethan's wife died. As one story goes, when plans were being made for taking her coffin to the church someone said, 'You could call on any of the neighbors to help. I'm sure there's not a man in town who wouldn't be glad to lend a hand.'

"A while later a twenty-four-year-old widow named Fanny came to stay in the Green Mountains."

"Oh-oh," Jack broke in. "This is going to get mushy. I can tell."

"Shut up!" Peggy hissed. "Ethan's going to get a date."

"Quiet! All of you!" Mrs. Ford snapped.

"Fanny's dead stepfather was a New Yorker and her dead husband was a British officer, which means Ethan shouldn't have wanted anything to do with her. But she was young and pretty and played the guitar. Her dead stepfather was a New Yorker and her dead husband was a British officer, which means *she* shouldn't have wanted anything to do with *Ethan*. Plus, he was more than twenty years older than she was and had three daughters. But he was also famous all over the country and had that original something that commands admiration, as Washington had said.

"One way or another, Ethan started visiting Fanny every day and Fanny let him.

"Either he wasn't on his best behavior with Fanny or she'd heard about his bad reputation. One day a man was talking with her about how Ethan was always hanging around where she was. He told her that Ethan was the most important man in the state.

" 'If you marry him,' he said, 'you'll be queen of Vermont.'

" 'And if I married the devil,' she replied, 'I'd be queen of hell.' "

Mrs. Ford gasped, which was sort of distracting. I'm sure that's why none of the others laughed.

"One morning in February 1784, Ethan stopped at the house where Fanny was staying.

" 'If we are to be married, now is the time, for I am on my way to Arlington,' he said to her.

" 'Very well. But give me time to put on my coat,' she replied.

"They were married that day by the chief justice of the Vermont Supreme Court, who asked, 'Do you, Ethan Allen, promise to live with Fanny Buchanan, agreeable to the laws of God?'

"And Ethan found himself in a bind. He had had trouble all his life living agreeably to anyone's laws, but he loved this young woman who, knowing his devilish nature, still wanted to be his wife. So he thought a moment and said, 'The law of God as written in the great book of Nature? Yes! Go on. My sleigh waits at the door.' "

As I had written those last words I'd thought about Ethan and Fanny riding off into the sunset in his sleigh. It was, I thought, a perfect ending. I imagined Mr. Santangelo saying something like, "It had everything! Comedy! Drama! Romance! Great job, Thérèse!" I believed I had real reason to hope for cheering and applause, or something nearly like it, anyway. Maybe a few people would ask me . . . beg me . . . to find out more and go on and on and on. As I finally finished writing my report all kinds of things ran through my mind.

Though it never occurred to me to picture Mrs. Ford tossing it into the metal basket on her desk and telling us that she was going to put a list of prepositions on the board for us to copy.

"Is she here? Is she watching me?" I kept asking Pokie during lunch. I was trying to chop up my meat loaf and shove it into my empty milk carton so Mrs. Ford wouldn't catch me with it.

"Too bad it's not cheese curds," Peggy said from the next table. "You'd gobble those right down, wouldn't you?"

The girls at her table all laughed as if they knew something really humiliating about me, though I was certain at least a couple of them had eaten their share of cheese curds. More, maybe.

"Don't worry. Mrs. Ford won't notice you're not eating your dog loaf. She isn't even here," Jack bellowed from his place.

I lifted my head and looked around. Mrs. Ford's old gray head was nowhere to be seen.

"Where do you suppose she is?" I asked Deborah when I went up to her and Yvette at recess. "Mrs. Ford," I added when she looked at me blankly.

"She must be inside," she answered in that calm, unshakable way I always used to love.

"Did you tell Yvette about the sledding party we're going to have next year?" I asked, more by way of reminding her about it, reminding her that we had plans, that I was somebody to her.

"Oh. Yes." She turned to Yvette. "Theresa and I thought we might try to have a sledding party next winter."

There was just the slightest stress on "might" and "try." It gave me something to think about while Deborah and Yvette were talking about summer camp.

I wandered over to where Jack and a couple of boys were picking on some girls who were jumping rope.

"You know," I said, "there's a story about Ethan walking all night in a circle to keep from freezing to death."

The girls looked at me as if I was embarrassing them somehow and started to move away.

I turned to Jack. "Ethan said he'd rather eat mouse meat than live under New York law."

"I want to hear more toilet tub stories," he broke in. "You got any more of those?"

"No," I said after thinking about it for a moment. "I don't think I have any more stories you'd like."

When we got into our classroom we found out why Mrs. Ford had skipped lunch duty. Our Vermont notebooks and our oral report materials were on our desks, many with new grades in Mrs. Ford's fine, even handwriting.

I picked up the stack of papers that made up all the different parts of my Ethan Allen report. There weren't too many marks on it—she'd just had the lunch hour, after all—but she'd had plenty of time to underline every "damn" with red ink and write "Poor taste" in several places. Underneath the grade she'd given me, she'd written, "You should have just written about Fort Ticonderoga. That's all you needed to do."

After I'd looked everything over, I picked up the papers and walked over to Mrs. Ford's desk.

"Oh, Theresa! Would you like to write the date on the board for this afternoon?" Mrs. Ford said when she saw me standing next to her.

"No. I wanted to show you this."

I held out the report. Mrs. Ford raised her eyebrows and frowned.

"I've seen it," she said grimly.

"You must not have known that I was supposed to get a B on it."

Mrs. Ford's mouth dropped. "How could you possibly think that?"

"Mr. Santangelo said that I was going to get a B. Everyone heard him."

I looked at my classmates. They all quickly looked away, trying to pretend they didn't see what was going on.

"I gave you a C because you did so much writing. I thought you deserved a little something for your effort. But this was not at all what I expect in an oral report," Mrs. Ford said.

"It has a narrative flow," I objected.

"A what?" Mrs. Ford laughed.

"It moves from a beginning to a middle to an end. It doesn't jump around in time. It's like a story. It's . . ."

"That was not the assignment."

"I read three books," I insisted. "I get Cs when I do nothing at all. I did so much . . ."

"But you did everything wrong," Mrs. Ford broke in. "You are supposed to learn from the lives of the great men. Your report was supposed to be on the hero of Ticonderoga. You should have done your report on the battle at the fort. That was what made Ethan Allen important."

"No, Mrs. Ford! That wasn't it at all! Hundreds of people have won battles at forts. What made Ethan important was . . . was . . . that he spoke for people. The farmers who were going to lose their land, the soldiers who died in those churches . . . no one would know about them if Ethan hadn't spoken up. He didn't have a fancy education or a lot of money, but lots of people didn't have those things. He spoke for them. That was the important part."

My voice was shaking. I could have just died.

"No, it wasn't," Mrs. Ford said as she handed me a piece of chalk and went back to marking some math papers. I stood there for a moment, waiting. I was sure that at any second I would hear someone behind me say, "But Mrs. Ford, there are natural, not teacher-made, laws, that everybody knows even if they're not written on the board. And those laws say that someone who worked as hard as Thérèse did and did as much as she did and did as well as she did has a right to a B." Or "We won't give up to tyrants our natural born liberties!" Or "The gods of the hills aren't the gods of the valleys," which wouldn't really fit the occasion any better than when Ethan first used it, but it came to mind because I'd just been talking about him.

Of course, none of that happened.

I went up to the blackboard, wrote "May 10, 1966," and silently headed back to my desk, still clutching my papers. Peggy grabbed me as I walked by her.

"It's May 8," she whispered. "Hurry and fix it. Maybe she won't notice."

I didn't care what the date was, and I didn't care if Mrs. Ford noticed. I just barely cared when, while I was standing next to Deborah waiting to get on the school bus, she said to me, "My father said that would happen."

"What would happen?"

"That when Mrs. Ford got back she would put you back in your place. He said it was wrong of Mr. Santangelo to encourage you to do more than you were able to do. It's cruel to let people get above themselves. Don't feel badly. It's not your fault. Oh! Time to go."

I stared as her line moved ahead of mine toward the buses. But what I was really seeing was Mr. Churchill the way he was the very first time I'd seen him at the library, looking so perfect, just the way anyone would want her father to look.

I got on my bus, sat in the seat I usually sit in, and slid across toward the window. I didn't look around until I heard someone drop down next to me. Good old Pokie, I thought.

But it wasn't good old Pokie who was there when I turned away from the window. Peggy was sitting there looking at me. I couldn't help it. I jumped.

"Deborah was just hanging around with you and Yvette hoping she could get one of you to convince your father to board a horse for her. It worked. Last night Mr. Morrissette called Mr. Churchill and said he'd do it. You probably won't see the inside of the Churchills' house again until Deborah wants something from you. Nobody does."

I nodded while I thought about what she said. "I feel kind of foolish but . . . thanks," I said.

"Okay, I've told you something, now you have to tell

me something. Were you the one who called *The Polka Hour* about my birthday?"

I smiled. "Yup."

Peggy closed her eyes and leaned back against her seat. "Thank goodness, it wasn't Pokie."

Marcel went right to the refrigerator when we got home and pulled out the bag of cheese curds. Mom was peeling potatoes at the kitchen sink. I took one look at her and started to cry.

"What's wrong?" she exclaimed, dropping her knife and rubbing her hands on her chest to dry them on a faded apron.

I threw my Ethan Allen report down on the table and headed out of the kitchen, stopping just long enough to stick my hand into the curd bag Marcel held out to me. Mom was flipping through my handwritten pages, groaning at the "Poor taste" comments, when I left for my bedroom.

I stretched out on my bed with my head turned so I could stare at one of those big ugly peonies. I could hear voices in other parts of the house, doors opening and shutting, a comedian telling a story on the television. But I didn't hear my father coming into my room.

"A C!" he said, sounding impressed. "My bébé has done it again, eh?"

I tried to laugh but just made a weird noise. "Yeah. I'll say."

He sat down on the edge of my bed, holding my report. "This is good. You know that, you?"

I closed my eyes and turned away.

" 'But Ethan was there,' " Dad said, looking down at my papers. " 'And he told those people that they should all think of those little girls as their own little girls, and they should feel the same pain and fear that their parents felt. And then he asked them if they could really give up and go home without making one more try to find those children, who might at that very moment be sobbing for their parents to rescue them.'

"You really wrote that?" he asked.

I just nodded.

" 'Grown men stood there and cried while they listened to Ethan. Then they went out one more time. And they saved those little girls.' "

He went on and on, and the sound of my own words was so good, to my ears, anyway, that I rolled over on my back in order to hear them better. Suddenly, I was surrounded by the smell of barn and cigarettes. And I realized that I knew that smell, not because it was barn and cigarettes, but because it was Dad. I couldn't help myself. I started to feel, if not actually better, at least at home and away from everything that was wrong.

We were there together, the two of us, for quite some time before I realized that the old man, he could read, him.

---

*E*than Allen and his wife Fanny would have three children together, joining his three surviving children from his first marriage. His son with Mary, his first wife, died while Ethan was a prisoner of war. A daughter also died while still young.

In 1785, Ethan published a second book, *Reason the Only Oracle of Man*, which described his religious views. Though there are occasional glimpses of the Allen wit here and there in the work, for the most part it is difficult reading. It was not well received by the public or critics.

Ethan retired from politics in 1787 and became a full-time farmer. He built a home near Burlington, Vermont. Once again, other family members moved north with him and lived nearby. In February 1789, a little more than five years after his marriage, Ethan and a hired hand took a sleigh to Ethan's cousin's farm to get hay. On the way back he died—or suffered an attack of some sort from which he died after returning home, depending on the account. He was only fifty-one years old.

Fanny Allen Hospital, in Colchester, Vermont, where

Aunt Joséphine received treatment, was named for Ethan's daughter Fanny, not his wife. The younger Fanny became a nun, an interesting occupation for an Allen child.

The Vermont Air National Guard, which Jack Thibodeau's brother belonged to, is known as "the Green Mountain Boys."

WIPS in Ticonderoga, New York, the radio station the LeClerc family is listening to when Roland first enters the story, is still broadcasting, though it no longer refers to itself as being "In the shadow of the great stone fortress."

And as for Ethan's first book, *A Narrative of Colonel Ethan Allen's Captivity*, it is still available today as *The Narrative of Colonel Ethan Allen*.

Sources used in researching the life of Ethan Allen include: Ethan Allen's *The Narrative of Colonel Ethan Allen*, *A Vindication of the Opposition of the Inhabitants of Vermont to the Government of New-York*, and *Reason the Only Oracle of Man*; Michael Bellesiles's *Revolutionary Outlaws: Ethan Allen and the Struggle for Independence on the Early American Frontier*; Dorothy Canfield Fisher's *Vermont Tradition*; Stewart H. Holbrook's *Ethan Allen*; and Jonathan Pell's *Ethan Allen*.

DISCARDED

DISCARDED